ADDICTED TO YOU

SWANSON COURT SERIES #2

SERENA GREY

WWW.SERENAGREY.COM

This book is a work of fiction. All names, characters, locations, and incidents are products of the author's imagination and have been used fictitiously. Any resemblance to actual persons, living or dead, locales, or events is entirely coincidental.

To everyone who ever picked up a book and was lost in the magic within.

ACKNOWLEDGMENTS

I am infinitely grateful to my readers for taking the chance with another one of my books. The fact that time and time again, you guys read and enjoy the stories I write—it means the world to me. Thank you for making my dream of writing come true for me.

There was a very long wait between the release of *Drawn to You*, the first book in this series, and this one. I'm so sorry for the delay, and I promise it WILL NEVER happen again for any subsequent books.

I'd like to thank my beta readers, Terri, Mary, Ashley—your feedback is invaluable. To the wonderful reviewers and bloggers who feed my confidence by telling me how much they're looking forward to receiving ARCs of my books, you guys are awesome.

To the love of my life, who reads everything I write, makes sure I have enough coffee and wine to fuel my creative process, kisses me with the same love and tenderness when I'm cranky from an editing session as when I'm actually being the hot sexy wife I promised you I'd be...I f***ing love you.

ADDICTED TO YOU

Rachel and Landon's story continues in this sequel to *Drawn to You*.

It was supposed to be just one week, just sex, no commitment, but somewhere along that overwhelmingly sexy ride, Rachel fell in love with Landon. There's just one problem—he doesn't do commitment.

As far as Landon knows, they have a good thing going, and he's not willing to let that go. Rachel can either tell him how she feels and watch him walk away, or keep it to herself and continue to drown in her feelings for him.

It hurts to be with him, but being without him hurts more. How do you make a choice about love when there's really no choice at all?

PROLOGUE

*A*IDAN is running around the playroom with his arms spread wide, making a whooshing sound like he's an airplane. His toys are all over the floor, but he manages not to trip on them. I'm on the sofa reading a comic book, and Sue is sitting by the window, close to my train set, with her nose stuck in a novel. She's Aidan's nanny, and all her books have drawings of people kissing on the covers.

I'd like to go downstairs, maybe to Mr. Hayes' office. He's the manager of our hotel, and sometimes he lets me walk beside him in the lobby when he greets the guests. He says the Swanson Court Hotel has a reputation for 'sterling' service, which means you have to give people what they want before they ask for it. Sue says I can't go downstairs because Mom will be back soon.

Aidan suddenly stops running and comes to peer at my comic book. I close the page I'm reading because there're zombies in it, and he's only four years old.

He makes a face and reaches for the book, and I stretch my hand up, holding it high enough so his fingers can't touch it.

"I wanna see," he complains, sticking out his lower lip.

Sue looks up at us. "Let him see, Landon," she says, frowning in my direction. She's really tiny, with short red hair like a boy's, and she just wants Aidan to be quiet so she can go back to reading her kissing book.

I start to think of a way to distract Aidan, but the door opens before I come up with anything.

"Mommy!" Aidan squeals, forgetting all about me as he runs toward her.

Mom scoops him up in her arms. "How's my darling little boy?" she says with a bright smile as Aidan settles his head on her shoulder. She buries her nose in his hair and sniffs before turning her smile to me and holding out a hand. "Landon, come say hi." Her voice is soft and gentle, like her, most of the time. Today, she's wearing a white, flowy suit, and her curly blonde hair is around her shoulders. She's beautiful. Everybody says so, even in the newspapers.

"Hi Mom." I get up and walk toward her outstretched hand, wondering if she'll let me go downstairs to Mr. Hayes. She ruffles my hair and smiles down at me. "Your dad is coming back tonight. Isn't that wonderful?"

I forget about going downstairs. "When is he coming?"

She shrugs. "He'll be here around seven in the evening, maybe."

I look down at my new watch, my grownup wristwatch—that's what my dad called it when he gave it to me before he traveled. "Five hours. Cool."

Mom laughs. I know she's happy too. My dad is away on business. He didn't travel so much before, but now he wants to expand our hotel, so he has to go to different cities. Sometimes, they fight on the phone, my mom and dad, especially when he's gone for very long. I heard Dad tell her she listens too much to the 'trash' people say. They were fighting when he said that, but they made up. They always make up when he comes back.

"Will Daddy tuck me in tonight?" Aidan asks.

"Of course," Mom tells him, chuckling. "They haven't been any trouble?" She's talking to Sue, who has quickly hidden her kissing book under some cushions.

"No, they've been rather sweet."

Mom looks at Aidan, who's still resting his head on her shoulder, looking as cute as an angel, then at the comic book I've tucked under my arm. Her eyebrows go up. She doesn't like the ones with zombies. "I doubt that," she replies with a sigh.

They start talking about something else then Donna, the maid, comes to the door holding the phone receiver. "Call for you, Mrs. Court," she says to my mom.

"Who is it?"

"Mrs. Buckley."

Mom sighs and sets Aidan on his feet before going to the door to take the receiver from Donna. Mrs. Buckley is mom's friend Auntie Thelma, who Mom laughingly calls a busybody. I don't like her, and I don't think Mom does very much either.

She takes the receiver with her, talking as she leaves us in the playroom. Aidan starts to run around again, singing a silly song he made up, so I leave him there with Sue and follow Mom to her sitting room. It's my favorite place in our whole apartment. It has billowy lace curtains, a reading nook with lots and lots of books, and a soft sofa that smells just like Mom.

She is standing by the windows with the receiver to her ear. "No, it's fine," I hear her say. "Thanks for telling me."

From the sound of her voice, I know something is wrong. She stands still for a few moments then starts to press the buttons on the receiver. When she puts it to her ear and starts talking again, her voice is angry, the way it always sounds when she's fighting with Dad.

"Someone saw you!" she says accusingly. "You had dinner with her and then you went upstairs together. Do you know how embarrassed I am? How am I supposed to believe you when the same thing keeps happening all the time?"

I don't understand everything she says, but I can tell she's mad at Dad. After a few more words, she tosses the receiver at the wall then puts her face in her hands as it clatters to the floor. She's sobbing loudly. I wish Dad would come home right now. He'll tell her he loves her and she'll be happy again.

"Mom?"

She spins around and sees me then quickly turns away again, but not before I see the tears on her face.

"Mom..." I try to think of something to say, one of the things Dad usually says to make her smile, but now I can't remember anything.

She wipes her eyes with the back of her hand.

5

When she turns around again, she's smiling. She doesn't want me to know she was crying, but I already saw, and her eyes are still red. "Hey sweetheart," she murmurs. "I thought you were in your playroom with Aidan."

"It's Aidan's playroom. I'm not a baby."

That makes her smile. "Okay."

I go to pick up the phone from the floor and place it on the coffee table. "You were fighting with Dad."

She smiles again. "Don't worry about it sweetheart. It was just..." She sighs. "It was nothing."

I nod. "He's coming home today," I remind her, hoping it will cheer her up. "You can make up when he gets here."

The smile disappears from her face. "No," she says, her voice changing. "By the time he comes, we'll be gone."

MOM IS SPEEDING. SHE HARDLY EVER DRIVES, except when we're at our house upstate and she doesn't want the chauffeur. She didn't want him today. She made Donna pack up a case each for Aidan and me, and she put them in Dad's green Ferrari and buckled us in the back.

Aidan is looking at me, his eyes wide. His tiny hands are tight around Alfred, his bear. Even he knows something is wrong. "Are we going to see Daddy?" he asks hopefully.

I can't think of anything to tell him, so I ruffle his hair. He likes that. "Where're we going?" I ask Mom.

She doesn't reply. We're already out of the city, but we're not going in the direction of our house.

"Where're we going?" I ask again.

"For God's sake," she snaps at me. "Keep quiet and let me drive."

"You're scaring Aidan," I tell her. I'm scared too. I don't want my parents to get a divorce.

Mom doesn't reply. Instead, she starts to drive faster, till it feels like we're flying over the highway.

Aidan peers out the window just as we zoom past a big truck. "Mommy?" he cries.

"Now you've upset him," Mom snaps.

I fold my arms. "I didn't upset him. You upset him."

"Landon..."

"I want to go back," I announce, hoping she'll turn around. "I want to wait for Dad."

She glares at me in the mirror, and I frown as deep as I can.

"Well, we're not going back," she says.

"I don't want to leave. If you're getting a divorce, I want to stay with Dad in the hotel."

"I want Daddy," Aidan cries.

Mom starts to cry. I can see the tears running down her face in the mirror. I know she really doesn't want to leave. If we go back and wait for my dad, everything will be okay.

But she keeps on driving, and I start to wish that anything would happen, anything at all to make us turn back.

CHAPTER 1

*G*OODBYE, *Rachel.*

Landon's last words to me before he drove away...they keep playing over and over in my head, and with every second that passes, I can feel the distance between us stretching, growing wider, triggering a frantic desire to run after him, to tell him I was wrong, that he's everything I want, everything I need.

You can't give me what I want.

Regret floods me, deep and painful, at the thought that I said those words to him.

I could have told him what I really wanted. I could have told him that I am in love with him, and I would have, but I knew what his reaction would be. He told me himself.

9

As soon as a woman starts to demand more than I can give, I walk away.

He would have walked away from me too, and I wouldn't have been able to bear it.

I did the right thing, I tell myself desperately. Being without Landon is a better option than being in love with a man who would never love me. Being without him is a better option than having to pretend that I don't want more than he does, that I'm not aching for something deeper.

Being without him is a better option than waiting helplessly for the day he'll tell me he's done with me.

Only right now, it doesn't feel like a better option. It feels like torture. It is agony, squeezing at my insides, tearing at my heart, and leaving scars I'm certain will never go away.

My memories don't help. Landon is everywhere in my head. The first time I saw him at the Swanson Court hotel, the elevator doors slid open to reveal the last thing I'd expected to see on the other side: a man with the physical perfection of a Greek god and such undeniable sexual magnetism. Without even touching me, he'd made me forget everything but how attracted to him I was. He thought I was a hooker, and I played along. The result was the most intense sexual experience of my life up to that point.

I remember Landon at his club, letting me think he still believed I was a hooker, then the next day in my boss's office... I almost smile at the memory. *"I want to fuck you again,"* he'd said. I'd been so angry, and yet, despite all my best intentions, I ended up in his office, half-naked on his desk, surrendering my body to his expert touch, letting him have his pleasure and taking mine, because when I was with him, it was impossible to deny that my body was totally his.

So many memories, all of them painful now-how long will it be before I stop thinking about him?

Staring unseeing at the door to my apartment, I wipe my eyes with the back of my hands. I have no idea how long I've been standing here, but I can't seem to bring myself to unlock the door, to step over the threshold and go on with life...life without Landon Court.

I wish I could find a way to erase the last thirty minutes. I want to avoid the aching emptiness growing inside me. I want, more than anything, to regain the physical connection and the pleasure of being with Landon—not the man everybody sees, the billionaire hotelier and ruthless businessman the press makes him out to be, but the man I'd glimpsed inside, the man Landon Court really is, the caring, sensual, and incredibly gorgeous man who, from the very first, made me feel things, both physical and emotional, that I never knew I was capable of.

The man I now have to live without.

Isn't this what you wanted? The voice in my head is harsh and taunting. Why else would you tell him you want more than he can give? Why else would you agree to meet with your ex? You wanted to show Landon you didn't care. You wanted to leave on your own terms, not as one of the women he had to walk away from because they wanted 'more than he could give.'

If it's what I want, then why is it tearing me to pieces?

Goodbye, Rachel.

"He can't give you what you want," I whisper to myself, trying to find even the slightest sliver of strength inside. "You're in love with him. He walks away from women who want commitment. You're doing the right thing ending it now."

The pep talk works somewhat. I take a deep breath and unlock the door to the apartment I share with my cousin Laurie. It's a small place, comfortably furnished, my home and sanctuary, and yet, right now all it does is remind me of Landon. He was only here a few times—to pick me up for a night at the theater, to spend the night with me, in my bed, drugging me with his touch, making me lose myself in the kind of pleasure only he could give—but he has left his mark somehow, the same way he's left a mark on my heart.

Closing the door behind me, I lean back on it and will my thoughts to find another direction, something else to focus on instead of Landon Court. At that moment, Laurie emerges from her room. She's already dressed for bed in a thigh-length t-shirt. The name of her boyfriend, Brett's gym is written on the front in big, bright lettering. Her curly hair is in a long braid, and as always, it's difficult to look at her without being reminded of how physically striking she is.

There is a touch of sadness on her face. It's been there since Brett told her they needed 'some time apart.' That and the t-shirt clue me in to the fact that she's probably having a bad day.

"You're back." She smiles, then she sees my face and the smile disappears. "Rach." Her voice rises in alarm. "What's wrong?"

Her concern makes tears rise in my eyes again. I'd like to tell her there's nothing wrong, because what's the point in compounding her pain with mine, but I've never been able to lie to Laurie. She knows me too well.

"Hi." My voice is shaky.

"What happened?" she asks, coming toward me.

I shake my head, words catching in my throat.

"Hey." Laurie puts an arm around me. "It's going to be okay, whatever it is."

No, it won't. "I need to lie down," I manage, pulling away and heading to the solace of my room. She follows me, watching from the door as I toss my bag on my chair and collapse crosswise on my bed, my eyes on the ceiling. In the dimness of the room, I give in to the tears, doing nothing to stop them from sliding down the side of my face.

"Are you going to tell me what happened?" Laurie's voice is gentle. "Did Landon do something?"

I don't answer. Inside, there is another surge of pain, followed by the now familiar temptation to go back to him and let him know that I was wrong, that I can't live without him and I don't want to try.

Goodbye, Rachel.

Laurie comes over to lie down beside me. She doesn't say anything, but the silence is soothing. We lie side by side for a long while, saying nothing. I wonder if she's thinking about Brett. The thought that we're both nursing broken hearts is infinitely depressing.

It was your choice to walk away, I tell myself, willing the tears to stop. It doesn't work. *I should be able to let him go*, I think miserably. We were never going to last forever anyway. We weren't even supposed to last this long. It should have been just one night. It should have ended the moment I walked out of his apartment without leaving my number.

It should have ended when we returned from that week in San Francisco. It should have ended before I got to the point where I fell so hard for him, but I'd wanted him too much, and he'd been so relentless in his seduction and in his unwillingness to let me go. Now, even though I've tried to convince myself that I can live with whatever part of himself he gives me, I know I can't. I want more. I'll always want more— more than he can give, more than he wants to give.

"I shouldn't have fallen in love with him," I say softly, breaking the silence in my room. My voice is still breaking, and my eyes are stinging. "It was too soon, and we agreed that it was going to be just sex."

"You don't get to choose when, or how, or with whom to fall in love," Laurie whispers, her voice gentle. "Sometimes it just happens and before you know it, you're reeling."

I am reeling. I draw in a shaky breath, fighting a new flood of tears. "After Jack, I should have learned to be more in control of my feelings. I don't want to be that girl who repeats the same mistakes with men." I'd thought I was in love with Jack Weyland, my ex. I still remember the hurt I felt when two years ago, Jack responded to my confession that I loved him with outright dismissal, but that hurt is nothing compared to the devastation I'm feeling now.

"Don't beat yourself up about it," Laurie sighs. "You fell for Landon, and there was an emotional connection. It's only natural that your feelings grew." She squeezes my hand. "What happened exactly? Do you want to talk about it now?"

As soon as a woman starts to demand more than I can give, I walk away.

I close my eyes. She warned me—what seems now like a long time ago—that I wouldn't be able to bear being in love and not knowing for sure that Landon felt the same. I swallow through the tightness in my throat. "I couldn't take it anymore, Laurie. I tried...but I just couldn't bear not knowing—or rather, knowing he would never allow himself to feel anything for me."

Laurie turns to her side, facing me. "Did you tell him you're in love with him?"

I shake my head. I've imagined telling Landon countless times. I've imagined confessing my feelings to him, but in my head, I always see his eyes cloud with pity and regret, and I hear his lips form the words to convey how sorry he is, how he doesn't feel the same.

"What would be the point?" I close my eyes.

"He'll just walk away, like he has from every other woman who ever wanted him to commit."

"You don't know that for sure," she points out.

"Actually, I do." I wish I didn't. I wish I could have stayed blissfully unaware that there was no point in loving Landon. I wish I didn't know, without a doubt, that our affair could only end one way—with Landon telling me he's done with me.

"So...you just left without giving him a reason?"

"No, I..."

You can't give me what I want.

I exhale softly. "I told him I wanted more than he was willing to give."

There's a long pause from Laurie. "But he doesn't know what you want exactly." She sounds confused. "And you've never bothered to ask him what he's 'willing' to give."

I don't answer.

"Rachel," she murmurs. "Do you ever think that maybe the fear of rejection is costing you more than anything you might lose if you're frank with him about your feelings?"

As much as I'd like to cling to the fantasy that telling Landon I love him would make any difference, I can't allow myself to be so foolish. I wipe my eyes with the back of one hand. "It's not the fear of rejection," I tell Laurie. "It's the reality of the man. I'd be a fool to continue to hope for a happy ending that's never going to happen."

"So that's it?" She sounds almost as sad as I am. "It's over?"

It's over. The finality of those words rip through my body, and I fight back the surge of panic. *It's over. It's over.*

"Yes," I whisper.

Laurie is silent. She squeezes my hand lightly. "I'm so sorry," she says gently. "But, I still think you should have told him how you feel. It's only fair that you let him know what you want from him."

I pull my hand from hers. "Maybe what I want is a man who would be willing to fight for me. Maybe I want a man who wouldn't walk away as soon as I indicate that I want something more from him, or accuse me of..." I trail off, my mind going back to Landon's reaction to my phone conversation with Jack.

Laurie rises from the bed and leans on her elbow.

"Accuse you of what?" she asks, clearly prepared to hate Landon on my behalf if he has dared to say anything unfair.

I sigh. I purposely kept silent about the part Jack played in my argument with Landon. Laurie's reaction to anything that involves Jack is never positive— not that I blame her. Right now I'm not feeling very good-natured toward Jack, even though nothing that happened tonight was his fault, really.

"Jack called me while we were on our way back," I admit. "He asked me to get a drink with him tomorrow, and I agreed. Landon didn't like it."

Laurie doesn't reply. Her dislike for Jack is intense, and she never pretended to support my friendship with him after he dumped me.

"I'm trying to understand," she says slowly, "but I can't. Why on Earth would you do that?"

I close my eyes. I've been torturing myself with the same question. "I don't know... Maybe I wanted a reaction. Maybe I wanted him to see that my life isn't all about hanging on to him, that I could walk away too, if I wanted."

"With Jack?" Laurie makes a frustrated sound. "Clearly you didn't get the reaction you wanted."

If you'd rather be with your ex, you don't have to conjure up vague reasons why we shouldn't be together. Just let me know and I won't stop you.

My eyes are aching with unshed tears, and right now, I just want to close them and try to forget everything. "Does it matter?" I sigh. "It's over anyway."

Laurie gets up from the bed and stands at the side, looking down at me with her hands on her hips. The light from the open door illumines her face, and I can see the frown of disappointment on her brow.

"I don't understand you, Rach." She walks to the door, and then comes back to the side of the bed. "If you want Landon to commit to a real relationship, why not just tell him?" She throws up her hands. "I don't know. Maybe deep inside, Jack is who you really want to be with."

"Don't be ridiculous, Laurie."

"Am I being ridiculous?" She snorts. "You let Jack keep you on a string for two years—two *years* of your fucking life. Now you're letting him come between you and Landon, who, from what I've seen, cares more about you than Jack ever did."

I don't have the energy to argue. "Laurie, this is not about Jack."

"From where I'm standing..." She makes a gesture of exasperation. "I don't know what kind of hold he has on you!" she exclaims. "Maybe you should call him now and tell him that you're available again, that you're still in love with him, and that you're ready to take whatever crumbs he throws your way. It's better than pretending you're ready to move on with someone else." She shakes her head. "I'm going to bed. Enjoy your date tomorrow."

I watch her stalk out of my room. She's so wrong about Jack, because he's the least important thing to me right now. I close my eyes and immediately, I see

Landon's face in my mind, hear his voice saying those words that make me want to weep.

Goodbye, Rachel.

I find a pillow to bury my face in and curl up into a ball. *You made the right decision*, I tell myself. *One day, you'll get over him.*

There's no consolation in that, and I'm still crying when I finally fall asleep.

CHAPTER 2

M Y sleep is laced with dreams about Landon, and more than once, I wake up in tears, only to continue tormenting myself with the memories. I can't silence the voice in my head telling me I've made a terrible mistake. I finally wake up tired, miserable, and almost late for work.

I shower hurriedly, tempted to remain beneath the flow of water and give it a chance to wash all my pain and memories away, but even if that would work, there's no time. I dress quickly in a white cotton blouse and a beige patterned skirt then brush my hair, despairing when my mind goes again to Landon, telling me how much he loved the color. *"Sometimes it's red,"* he'd said. *"Sometimes gold, and sometimes it's both."* I breathe shakily, unable to suppress the memory of his fingers in my hair.

Frustrated, I drop the hairbrush and clip the strands away from my face, foregoing any attempt at makeup, even though my eyelids show evidence of all the crying I did last night. I wince at my reflection but decide there's nothing I can do.

Laurie has already left for work, which is fine with me; I'm not eager to talk to her after her reaction last night. I hurry out of the empty apartment, hoping I'll find a cab before too long.

Outside, there's the sparse morning crowd from my street—a few people on the tree-shaded sidewalk hurrying to work, others pushing little kids in strollers, and a few cars parked on the street. I clear the steps of the building entrance and the small paved area between the sidewalk and the building before I notice the familiar black sedan parked on the curb.

My steps falter. Something builds in my stomach, a mixture of dread and anticipation that seizes my body and makes me unable to keep moving. I watch, barely breathing, as the rear door opens and Landon steps out of the car.

A soft breath escapes from my lips, and my eyes close, almost reflexively, a protective measure to prevent me from going to pieces just from looking at him. Yearning courses through my body like a tidal wave, drowning my heart and weakening my knees. I'm suddenly shaking, my whole body drawn to him like a moth to a flame.

What is he doing here?

I take a deep breath, and when I open my eyes again, he's still there. His eyes are burning with that familiar cobalt intensity, provoking an answering flame deep in my belly. I blink back a sudden wave of tears. The last thing I need is to be so close to his devastating beauty. Already, my eyes are greedily devouring him. The burnished gold of his hair is gleaming in the early morning sun, the waves framing and emphasizing the raw perfection of his face, and he's dressed to conquer the world in an exquisite deep blue suit, one that does nothing to hide the powerful body beneath.

In the few seconds I spend looking at him, I get the feeling that if I walked into his arms, last night wouldn't matter anymore, only how much I want him, and how much he wants me. For a moment, I'm tempted to do just that, to forget all my doubts and just be with him.

But for how long?

It takes an effort to tear my eyes away from his

perfection, to break the spell he has me under. He takes a step toward me. "Hello." His voice is low and washes over me like a familiar, much-desired caress.

Suddenly the back of my throat feels raw. I swallow hard. I'm not going to start crying again. *I chose to walk away*, I remind myself. It was my choice.

There is some oncoming foot traffic on the sidewalk, so I have to step out of the way. I move toward the curb, closer to where Landon is standing. "What are you doing here?" I ask, my voice thick and rough.

He looks closely at my eyes, and I wonder how obvious it is that I spent the night in tears. A small frown touches his brow, and I can tell he hasn't missed a thing. He starts to come closer to me, and the slight movement instantly raises my heart rate. I flinch and he stops himself, instead thrusting his hands into his pockets and rocking on his heels.

His voice is low and quiet. "I wanted to talk."

I shake my head. My commitment to staying away from him is so shaky that I don't trust myself to spend enough time with him to 'talk.' "I'm late for work," I tell him, hoping that will be sufficient for him to leave me alone.

He takes a step toward me, closing the small distance between us. I pull in a breath, and my senses are assaulted by all the familiar scents—the faint whiff of his cologne, the delicious hint of soap and shampoo... I breathe, concentrating on the small frown he still has on his face. "I'll take you to your office," he suggests. "We can talk in the car."

I contemplate sharing that small space with him, and I shake my head again. "No. Thanks."

His quick intake of breath is followed by a frustrated hand running through his hair. "Rachel," he says, his voice a study in patience. "Why are you making this so hard?"

It became hard the moment I fell in love with you, I say silently. Behind me on the sidewalk, people walk past us, and it makes me think how awkward we must look, just standing on the street.

"Fine," I concede, walking past him to the car. I slide to the far side and adjust my skirt while I wait for him to join me. Landon's preferred chauffeur, Joe, is behind the wheel, his crew cut visible from the back.

"Good morning, Joe," I greet, my voice sounding churlish even to me.

"Good morning, Miss Foster," Joe replies cheerfully.

The door closes with a barely audible click as Landon joins me at the back, and before the car starts to move, Joe plugs in a pair of earbuds. I fix my gaze out the window, determined to resist the urge to feast my eyes on Landon's perfection, but every nerve in my body is aware of him, right beside me, so close, so gorgeous, so...everything I want.

You're in love with him, I tell myself, trying to be sensible. He doesn't feel the same way, and there's absolutely no chance he ever will. He can't give you what you want, and you know he'll only hurt you in the long run.

But...what could ever hurt more than leaving him hurts now? Temptation whispers the words in my head, and I do my best to ignore them. *I'm doing the right thing for me*, I assure myself. Why postpone the pain that will surely come? Why keep holding on to a man who'll only want me for a short while?

The car joins the traffic heading toward Midtown, and I'm so acutely aware of Landon, of the waves of sensual energy coming from his body and the desire growing low in my belly. I'm almost afraid to move. The silence stretches, along with my nerves.

"You're still going out with Weyland tonight?"

The question makes me turn to look at him. He's facing straight ahead, his fingers splayed on his lap. His body looks as stiff as mine feels. I close my fists, fighting the ache in my fingers from my desire to touch him, to feel the skin of his face, to smooth the silk of his hair...to allow my heart to win over my head.

Instead, I respond to his question. "Is that what you wanted to talk about?"

He doesn't reply.

I turn back to the window. The truth is, I'm in no mood to see Jack, especially considering the state of my emotions at the moment. Jack had warned me about falling in love with Landon. It had been ridiculous and presumptuous coming from him, but still, if he caught any inkling that things were not perfect, he would take it as proof that he'd been right.

"I don't know," I murmur. "I already told him I would."

There is another long silence, and I wonder what he's thinking. I steal a glance at him and catch him looking at me.

"What did Weyland say to you at the Swanson Court, the day we met?"

The question takes me by surprise, and I shake my head, confused. "I don't think that has anything to do with—"

"Please," Landon stops me. "Rachel, I'm trying to understand your...relationship with him, and why he keeps coming up between us."

Us. Such a small word, but at that moment, it almost destroys me. I breathe. "I don't think it makes

SERENA GREY

any difference..." I stop talking, the intense burn in
Landon's eyes telling me he won't stop until I tell him
the truth. "He told me he was engaged," I say quietly.

Landon nods. "You were in love with him."

It's a statement, not a question. I don't reply. I'd
thought I was in love with Jack, but I was wrong.
What I'd felt for Jack at the time was nothing
compared to the emotions coursing through me now.

Landon isn't done. His eyes are still on mine,
searching and demanding answers. "Tell me what
happened between you two."

It doesn't matter, I say silently. *It ceased to matter the
moment those elevator doors opened and I saw you standing
there.* "I met him when I went to work at Gilt. We
started seeing each other, and we stopped after about
two months." I shrug. "But we stayed friends."

"Why did you stop seeing each other?"

"We didn't want the same things."

Landon chuckles, but he doesn't sound or look
amused. "You're being deliberately vague."

"I told him I was in love with him." I turn back to
the window, escaping the force and beauty of the eyes
trained on me. "He didn't feel the same way."

There is another silence from Landon. Is he
wondering why I remained friends with Jack after
that? Why two years later I was still so into him that
I cared that he was getting engaged to someone else?

Does it make him think less of me? Not that I should care what he thinks—after all, I'm supposed to be getting over him.

"You told me you were completely over Weyland," Landon says, his voice low. "Were you being honest?"

If he only knew. I close my eyes, pushing away the pain threatening to engulf me. "There's really no point in talking about Jack."

He is silent. I listen to his fingers beat a low, erratic rhythm on the tops of his thighs. "Are you still in love with him?" I hear him say, his voice grave.

I consider saying yes. The idea cycles through my head, and I contemplate what would follow. Landon would walk away. There's no way he'd keep pursuing me if he thought I was in love with someone else. He'd let me go, and no matter how miserable that would make me, at least I'd have the space I need to get over him.

But I can't bring myself to lie to him. There's something in his eyes, some emotion that reaches deep inside me and makes me want to remove every single doubt in my mind, to break down every single wall I've labored to put up between us. I pull in a shaky breath. "No," I whisper softly. "I was never in love with him. For a while, I thought I was, but I was mistaken."

31

Landon releases a long breath then leans toward me, a puzzled frown on his face. "Then why?"

His face is so close to mine that it's difficult to think. My eyes slip to his lips, and I have a sudden memory of those lips on my skin, tasting, teasing... I swallow. "Why what?"

He covers my hand with his, the touch firm but gentle. I start to tremble, knowing he only has to keep touching me and I'll fall to pieces. I try to pull my hand away, but he holds on, bringing his other hand to keep mine between both of his. His next words are tender and probing. "Why do you keep pushing me away?"

I try to remember all the reasons, but everything is clouded by my desire to give in, to forget my doubts, to surrender myself to him, for the pleasure...

...and the inevitable pain.

"Because I don't want this," I whisper. "I don't want to be with you." *Not like this*, I add silently. *Not unless you love me too.*

His eyes close, and his jaw flexes. I don't wait for him to say anything before I continue, digging my heels in before I surrender to the temptation to tell him how I really feel, what I really want. "I meant it when I said you can't give me what I want."

Something like pain flashes in his eyes, but I can't be too sure. I watch his throat work as he swallows then releases my hand, letting it fall back on my thigh. The thought that I've hurt him is almost unbearable. I want to take it back, but I know he'll get over it. He'll find some other woman who will be happy without the promise of commitment, or will at least pretend to be.

My eyes are stinging with tears, and I blink them away, looking straight ahead to keep Landon from noticing. If only I didn't love him so much, didn't want him so much...

I'm relieved when I see the Gilt building a few yards ahead. We're both silent as the car inches forward in the traffic. It seems to take forever till Joe slides up to the curb at the entrance and stops.

I risk a glance at Landon. He doesn't look at me, and his face is as remote and distant as if it was hewn from stone. "I... Thanks for the ride."

His response is a small, bitter chuckle. "I should thank you," he says, "for making it clear to me, without any doubt, that I can't always get what I want."

I flinch at his tone, and at the realization that he thinks I've been trying to teach him a lesson. Taking one last, long look at his beautiful profile, I decide that there would be no point in arguing.

My heart is heavy as I leave the car. With my whole body trembling, I take the steps up toward the glass doors. I hear the low purr of the engine as the car starts to move away, but I don't look back.

I'm doing the right thing, I tell myself for the thousandth time.

It only makes me feel worse.

CHAPTER 3

"*I*T *has taken a lot of work to restore the hotel's faded charms—an acclaimed refurbishment team, for one, all of whom do not hesitate to give the real credit to one man, the new owner. From the Italian marble in the lobby, the exquisite mosaic in the indoor swimming pool, the extensive art collection, to the crested stationary, and even the cutlery, everything you find at the Gold Dust, the newest addition to the Swanson Court Hotels, has been carefully chosen by Landon Court himself. The man behind the contemporary success of the Swanson Court Brand isn't just a hotelier; he knows what he wants, and he never hesitates to go after it.*"

Chelsea looks up from her tablet, her eyes sparkling with amusement as she raises an eyebrow in my direction. Like me, she's a features associate at

35

Gilt Travel. She's also disarmingly pretty, and genuinely friendly. Today, she's wearing all blue, her corn-silk hair in a loose ponytail. "Could it be any more obvious that you're in love with this man?" she teases.

I busy myself with powering on my computer, Landon's voice still sounding in my ears.

Why do you keep pushing me away?

After this morning, after our conversation, I'm suddenly more confused and unsure of myself. As if that's not enough, the new issue of Gilt Travel has been electronically delivered to subscribers and staff, along with my article about the Gold Dust. Everyone wants to tell me how good it is, but the more I have to talk about it, the harder it is to stop thinking about its subject.

Why do you keep pushing me away?

The effort it takes to force the image of him from my mind is almost paralyzing.

"I'm not in love with him," I tell Chelsea without taking my eyes off my computer screen. There's nothing on the screen, but I don't want her to see the lie on my face.

Chelsea is still laughing, oblivious to my inner torment. "That's what they always say."

I don't reply. I type in my password and concentrate on my screen as it comes to life. I search the files for something…anything I can start working on, anything to make me stop thinking.

Chelsea stops laughing, sensing that something is wrong. She steps toward my desk and gives me a sharp look. "You're not seeing him anymore."

I close my eyes, and even then all I can see in my head is Landon.

Why do you keep pushing me away?

I focus on Chelsea, pushing everything else out of my mind. "It wasn't supposed to be a permanent thing." I meet her eyes and force a brightness into my voice that I don't feel, which, I'm sure, does little to deceive her.

She sighs. "Are you doing okay?"

I'm sure that as soon as she leaves my office, I'm going to succumb to the tears stinging in my eyes. "I'm fine," I lie.

It's obvious she doesn't believe me. "We should go out," she suggests after a short silence. "Let's pick a night, hit the clubs, and party till we forget that men exist. Me, you, Laurie, Sonali too, if she's done with her juice cleanse by then. It'll be great."

I nod vaguely. *Laurie.* With the distraction of Landon's appearance this morning, I've not had the chance to dwell on her reaction from last night. Now that I'm reminded, it rankles. I understand why she lost her temper over Jack. She nursed me through two years of crying over him, but her accusations were so fucking unfair.

When Chelsea finally leaves me alone, I abandon my desk and any attempt to work and walk over to the small window. My view is limited to a small slice of sky and some other buildings, their reflective glass walls hiding the busy people inside them.

I close my eyes, wondering where Landon is, what he's doing. He's probably at his office by now, acquiring more properties and making more money. Did I succeed in driving him away? Is it possible that he's also thinking about me? Did I leave some sort of indelible mark in his life too? Will he be distracted at his desk by the memory of tearing my clothes off right on that same surface and making me come over and over?

That particular memory is followed by a surge of desire, and raw heat unfurls between my thighs. *It's just sex*, I tell myself, leaning my head on the glass, hoping the cool surface will help to calm my raging hormones and emotions. *It's just sex, and he's just a man.*

A man I'm in love with.

I have to stop thinking about him or I'll go mad, or go to him and beg for his love, or accept whatever part of himself he's ready to give, for however long.

I'm ashamed how attractive that option seems. It's not fair. I want to have love in my life. I want something like what my parents have. I want a man who'll give up everything if he has to, just so we can be together.

And I want that man to be Landon.

Pushing away from the window, I return to my desk. Just as I reach my seat, there's a soft knock on the door. A moment later, it opens, and Jack Weyland enters my office.

He pauses at the door, a smile on his face. Looking at him, it's easy to see why I was stuck on him for two years. He's charming and funny, and though he's not as tall or as perfectly built as Landon, he has a slim, fit physique, like a model's. With his cloudy gray eyes, black hair, and the perfect smile he never hesitates to use, he's unquestionably handsome. He's also the most famous writer at Gilt Travel.

Today, he's wearing a dark vest over a lightly striped shirt. Dark pants show off his slim hips and long legs. His hair is mussed, pushed back, with one curly forelock falling onto his forehead. He looks good, and it's obvious that he knows it.

"Hey beautiful," he says, making it sound as if he's been waiting to see me all morning, as if I've just made his day by existing. It must be a gift, I think, how he can flatter and seduce with only a few words.

"Hi Jack." I force a smile, determined to hide the fact that a moment before he came in, I was struggling under the weight of my emotions, and I still am —not that I care what he thinks, but I'd rather walk a plank than give him a reason to think he'd been right to warn me about Landon.

He walks over to my desk and leans his hip on the edge. "I read your article," he says. "Nice work."

The article again. I have to force myself not to succumb to the reminder of Landon. "Thanks, though I'm surprised you had the time. No new assignments?"

He grins. "You know I always have time for you."

Since when? Definitely not during the two years I spent waiting, hoping, being there for him while he went from one exotic beauty to another. It's almost as if he's forgotten that he knowingly toyed with my feelings for far too long.

He's peering at my face, and I quickly turn my gaze to the surface of my desk. I'm not as happy as I'd prefer for him to think, but I'd rather he didn't see the evidence on my face. "You said you caught a bug?" I ask, remembering what he'd said on the phone.

"Yeah." He nods. "I was out for a couple of days. I'm great now. Just missing my favorite person in the world."

Our old joke. I ignore it. "I'm glad you're okay."

He sighs. "I stopped by to remind you about tonight."

I should tell him I've changed my mind. I look from the hip casually perched on my desk to his familiar smile, and I imagine how a few months ago I would have been so glad, so grateful to have his attention.

"Why, Jack?"

He frowns. "Why what?"

"First you surprise me in San Francisco, now you want to go out. A few weeks ago you were engaged, and you wanted me to be happy for you. Now you're suddenly eager to spend time with me."

"We always spent time together," he says with a shrug. "Even as friends." There's a pause. "I always looked forward to your company, no matter who I was seeing or what I was working on, Rachel. That should never be in doubt."

He'd wanted my company, but not my love, for two years. Now there's Landon, who wants my body, but would never allow himself to love me. It feels like I'm the cursed girl in a warped fairy tale. "It's never going to be the way it was," I tell Jack, thinking about those months spent as his loyal, adoring sidekick, the long months spent hanging on to his every word, hoping that one day he would realize he was wrong to throw my love back in my face.

He looks pained. "Because I got engaged? Or

because your boyfriend would likely swoop in and cart you away like you're his property?"

He's referring to the night in San Francisco, when Landon interrupted our date. I almost smile at the memory. Jack is waiting for me to reply, but before I can, there's another knock on the door. It's soon followed by one of the interns carrying in a bouquet of purple lilies and yellow orchids in a beautiful glass globe.

"These were delivered for you," she says, managing to simper at Jack while she places the flowers on my desk. Half the girls in the building are crazy about him, and obviously she's one of them.

"I'm Meredith," she tells him, starting to describe an article of his that she 'really liked.' He answers her politely, his lack of interest painfully obvious. He never dates any of the girls from Gilt. I was his one exception, and for a long time, I told myself it was because we had something special.

Now I couldn't care less.

After Meredith finally leaves, Jack looks from the flowers to my face, his eyebrows raised questioningly.

I ignore him. My heart is already racing, and I know, without reading the card, who sent the flowers. Why would he do that? Especially after this morning? I don't need any more reminders, any more reasons to cry. I suddenly wish the flowers would disappear, along with every torturous memory of Landon Court.

"Aren't you going to see who they're from?" Jack asks. There's a tightness in his voice that wasn't there before.

I'd rather not. I'd rather ignore them and pretend I don't care, but with Jack here, I can't do that. My hand trembles as I reach for the card, pulling it out of the plastic stick to read the words in Landon's hard, slanted handwriting.

Great Article.

That's all it says. Nothing else. I remember his face from this morning, the flash of emotion when I told him once again that he can't give me what I want.

Why do you keep pushing me away?

Slowly, I stroke a finger over the velvety surface of the card, overcome by an intense, painful yearning. *You'll regret walking away from him*, a reproachful voice accuses in my head. *You've made a huge mistake in letting him go.*

"From Court?"

I blink at Jack, realizing I'd almost forgotten he was here. Hastily, I drop the card on my desk, ashamed of how easily I'd been affected by just flowers and a card. In the space of a few moments, I'd almost forgotten all the reasons why I walked away in the first place.

"Yes." I clear my throat and give Jack a small half-smile. "They're from Landon."

"Getting serious?" His eyes are questioning.

No, actually it's over. I don't say that. Instead, I give him a tired look. "Are you going to warn me again? About how heartless he is with women, how I shouldn't fall in love with him?"

"No." He shakes his head. "I believe you'll find out for yourself."

I lower my eyes to my desk. *I won't find out*, I think silently, *because I've already left him.* "Come on Jack," I say with a lightness I don't feel. "You have more important things to do with your time than to speculate about my private life."

He doesn't miss a beat. "What's more important than you?"

I roll my eyes and he laughs, then his face turns serious. "Rachel, I hope you know that I'm here for you, whenever you need me."

He looks so sincere. I sigh, looking from his face to the flowers on my desk. They're exquisite, and they'll make me think of Landon all day. When I get home, he'll be there too, in my memories, in Laurie's silent disapproval... I have nowhere to escape him.

"So tonight...?" Jack prompts with a hopeful

smile, interrupting my thoughts. "Please don't tell me you've changed your mind."

I look into his gray eyes, the familiar smile, and that lock of hair flopping onto his forehead. Hopefully, the few hours I spend with him will not be full of thoughts of Landon.

~

"WELL…" I SMILE. "AT LEAST TELL ME WHERE WE are going.

AFTER Jack leaves, I throw myself into my work, emailing drafts to the features editor, replying to my emails, and checking social feeds for interesting ideas. By the time I leave the office, I'm mentally exhausted.

I have a dinner reservation at Angelos, a Greek restaurant we've included in an article about places to eat Greek in major cities. In the cab on my way over there, my mind slowly loosens from the whirl of the day and inevitably goes back to Landon.

Why did he send the flowers? Was he trying to tell me something? Was it a final footnote, a small gesture to mark the end of our affair? I can't pretend to understand his motives, especially after this morning.

The flowers were probably nothing, I decide

finally, something he had already planned and decided not to cancel. They'll probably be the last personal communication we'll ever have, leaving me with only my thoughts to conquer. Maybe one day I'll run into him at an event, or at a restaurant. Maybe by that time I'll be over him, and I won't completely fall apart.

At Angelos, a waiter leads me to a table. The restaurant is quiet, with only a few diners. At my table, I settle into a cushioned seat set against one of the white brick walls and go through the menu, deciding on the roast fish and vegetables with the signature custard cream pastry.

The food is superb, and I haven't eaten all day, so for a few moments, I concentrate only on the taste and flavor. Later, I type a few notes in my phone while sipping the remaining wine from the glass I ordered. At one of the other tables, a woman laughs at something her companion said then takes the forkful of food he offers her. I turn away, my chest suddenly tightening. How long will it take until the ache goes away?

My phone vibrates. It's a text from Jack.

Where are you?

On my way, I text back before gathering my things. Outside, I hail a cab to take me to the bar where we've agreed to meet. The cabbie soon leaves me on the sidewalk in front of the incongruous wooden doors that are the entrance to Ambrosia. It's an art bar with a constant exhibition of paintings and a stage for presentations, which, right now, is empty.

I spot Jack at the bar. He's deep in conversation with a good-looking woman with short, messy hair and bright red lipstick. I watch him as he says something to make her laugh. He leans forward, smiling at her. Does he even know what he's doing? Or is flirting just his default setting? I walk over to join them. "Hi Jack."

He turns to me, and his smile widens. "Here you are." He leans in to kiss my cheek, and I can't help but notice that the long day hasn't diminished his good looks. "I got us a table," he tells me before turning back to the woman and saying something that sounds like 'Nice to meet you.'

I follow him to one of the booths set back from the main bar, and he beckons for one of the hovering waiters. "You look great, by the way."

I'm wearing the same thing I was wearing in the morning. "You already saw me today," I remind him after putting in my drink order.

"So what?" he says, his grin unrepentant. He pushes his hair back from his forehead and leans forward. "I wasn't sure I told you earlier."

I chuckle. "Flattery won't get you anywhere."

47

"So." He leans back. "What will?" The grin has disappeared, replaced by a measuring gaze.

I ignore the question. I have no intention of going down that road with him, not now, not ever.

"Seriously," he insists. "What will get me somewhere with you?"

"Leave it, Jack," I say softly. My eyes linger on his handsome face for a moment, and suddenly I'm flooded with gratitude toward Landon. I'm grateful that maybe because of the time we spent together, I can look at Jack and feel nothing. I can spend time with him without being reduced to a nervous bundle of expectation.

"You want to eat anything?" he asks. "They have…" He shrugs. "Stuff."

I shake my head. "I already had dinner."

He grins. "I remember when you'd order a little of everything so you could taste it all. You were fearless."

A trip down memory lane? I smile despite myself, remembering those early days with him. I was fearless until I mentioned that I was in love with him and he made me feel like a fool.

Our drinks arrive. Jack sips his while watching me, a thoughtful frown on his face. On the small stage, a scruffy looking guy appears with a sheaf of papers in his hand. Someone brings him a chair and a mic then he sits and introduces himself before starting to read a poem.

A few people are listening, but most carry on with their conversations and their drinking. The poem is really lengthy and seems to be about someone being torn away from his dreams. The tone reminds me too much of how I feel, how torn up I am inside, so I try not to listen.

"Oh well," Jack says when the guy finishes, leaving the stage to halfhearted applause. "That was sad."

"Yes, it was." I take a small sip of my drink. "So, when and what is your next assignment."

He shrugs nonchalantly. "I'm liking just being in the city right now."

I raise a brow. "That is so unlike you. What happened to your wanderlust, your adventurous spirit?" His only reply is another shrug. I frown, puzzled. "How long are you going to stay this time?"

He looks at me, his gray eyes suddenly sober and intense. "How long do you want me to?"

I sigh. "It's never depended on me before."

He takes another sip from his glass then lets his eyes wander around the bar before dragging them back to me. "Maybe now it does."

Three months ago, I would have been overjoyed to hear words like that coming from him, but now...

Now...

My brain rebels against the thought, trying to suppress it, but I can't. It bursts, uncontrollably, to the surface.

Now, I'm in love with Landon.

I draw in a breath and concentrate on Jack's face, doing my best to purge every thought of Landon from my mind. *Someday*, I tell myself. *I'll look at his face and feel as little as I feel right now with Jack. I'll look at him and be unable to remember the intensity of the emotions now raging inside me.*

It's very unlikely, and there is a sense of loss at the thought of letting go of my feelings for Landon, but what choice do I have?

Jack is looking at me, waiting for a response.

I sigh. "Jack." My voice is gentle. "You have to let it go."

"Because of *him*?"

"Yes, and also because of *you*. I got over you Jack. Let it go."

He draws in a sharp breath. "I'm trying to."

We're both silent. It starts to feel uncomfortable, and I begin to think that maybe I should leave.

"My mother's back in town," Jack says.

"Really?" I give him a concerned glance. I've never met his mother, but I know who she is. Gertrude Weyland wrote a novel in her early twenties, which, more than thirty years later, has never gone out of print. After that one book, she stopped writing and went to work in publishing. She's been living in London working as an editor with one of the big publishing companies. All through my years of knowing Jack, he hardly ever mentioned her. From the few times he did, I got the feeling they didn't have a good relationship, but I never pressed for the details.

"Is she staying?" I ask.

"I don't know." He frowns. "I haven't seen her."

He doesn't look like he wants to either. "Will you?" I ask, wondering how bad their relationship must be for him to be so hesitant. I've always been able to take my relationship with my parents for granted. I've never had cause to doubt their love and unwavering support. It's hard for me to understand anyone not being able to enjoy the same kind of relationship with their parents.

Jack shrugs. "I have to." He downs his drink and signals for a waiter. "Will you come with me?"

"Me?" I shake my head in surprise. "Why?"

He sighs. "She and I..." He shakes his head, and there's no sign of the easy charm that's usually a part of his every word and expression. "It would be great to have someone else there."

I pause to think. A few months ago, I would have been excited, both at the thought of meeting

Gertrude Weyland and by the fact that she is Jack's mother. I'd love to meet the woman, but with Jack? I'm not sure.

However, considering it against the bleak hours I have stretched out in front of me, filled with the memories of Landon that I can't escape, it doesn't seem like such a bad idea.

I sigh. "When?"

"Tomorrow evening." He looks grateful. "Or the day after. I've stayed away this long, what's a few more days?"

WE SPEND THE REST OF THE EVENING TALKING about stuff from the office. To my relief, Jack doesn't venture back into the territory of exploring his feelings for me, whatever they are. It's almost like old times, except somehow, it's obvious that we both have a lot on our minds.

When I'm ready to leave, Jack helps me find a cab. In the rearview mirror, I see him standing on the curb watching the cab silently, and the image makes me inexplicably sad.

My phone vibrates, and I fish it out of my bag. There is an alert for one of my many reminders, and also two missed calls from Landon.

My breath catches. I stare at his name on the screen, my stomach knotting hard. First his appearance this morning, and now phone calls. It all points to one thing: that he's as reluctant to let me go as he was when he convinced me to go with him to San Francisco.

The thought is as alarming as it is exciting. A wave of anticipation and expectation floods over my skin, almost sexual in the effect it has on me. I close my eyes and lock the screen before tossing the phone back into my bag and searching for other things to crowd my head with. Work, even Jack—everything is safer than thinking about Landon.

The cabbie leaves me outside my apartment building and a few people walk past me, talking and laughing, probably on their way to one of the many clubs on the next street. One of the guys whistles at me, but I ignore him and he goes back to laughing with his friends. I'm about to head for the doors when something catches my attention across the tree-lined street.

The silver Jaguar is parked directly opposite from where I'm standing, in the same spot Landon parked the night he came over and called me from his car. A tremor moves slowly up my spine, especially when the pleasurable memories from that night flood my head. *It could be anyone*, I tell myself, my eyes still on the familiar car. There are probably multiple silver Jaguars in my neighborhood alone.

But it is Landon.

I watch him step out of the car, his unmistakable lithe form circling around it until he's standing directly opposite me on the other side of the street. He's wearing a dark sweatshirt and jeans. At first glance, apart from his searing hotness, he doesn't look much different from any of the new grads in my neighborhood—but when he moves, there's something in the way he carries himself, something that points to the fact that beyond the wavy, dark gold hair, the beautifully sculpted face, and the sexy frame, there's the enigmatic and powerful man beneath, the billionaire owner of the Swanson Court hotels.

What does he want now?

I stand there frozen. We're looking at each other, silent, but my heart is pounding, my skin heating, my whole body drowning with painful longing. How am I supposed to get over him when just the sight of him renders me confused, aching, and full of desire?

Angry with myself—and with him for making me feel so helpless—I turn around sharply, stalking toward the entrance to my building.

"Rachel," I hear him call, but I don't answer. I'm too angry and afraid of what will happen if I let him come too close.

With a few long strides, he catches up to me at the door.

"For God's sake Rachel. Why are you running?"

I don't look at him, but I can feel him, so close. His whole body is like a magnet, pulling me helplessly toward him. My hands are shaking, the aching hole in my heart widening painfully. I close my eyes, willing myself to be strong. I want to reach for his face and kiss him, I want to press my body to his and feel the way he wants me. My head fills with possibilities and images of us, bodies entwined, in his car, maybe, or upstairs in my bed.

I try to breathe, to dispel the erotic images from my mind before turning to face him. "Maybe because you seem to be stalking me," I reply, my voice surprisingly steady.

His beautiful lips move in something like a smile, and yearning floods my chest. *I can't do this*, I realize. *I want him too much.* "Landon." My voice is a whisper. "You should leave."

"Why?" There is so much to the question. I don't know how to reply, so I don't. He makes an exasperated sound in his throat. "How was your *date*?" he asks bitterly.

"You came all the way over here to ask me that?" I pause. "Or did you come to make sure I didn't end up in Jack's bed? That's why you called earlier isn't it? To make sure that even though I was with him, I wouldn't forget about you?" I fold my arms and glare at him. "Because you're what, jealous?"

My outburst seems to amuse Landon. He leans toward me. "Of course I am," he whispers.

His face is so close, his vibrant eyes, his incredibly sensuous mouth. I lick my lips, an involuntary movement that he doesn't miss. His eyes follow the motion with a fierce hunger that draws a reaction from my core. I close my eyes and breathe. *He doesn't feel the same way you feel about him*, I tell myself desperately. *He'll never love you the way you want him to.*

"Go away," I whisper.

He moves even closer. "No."

I look away from his face, reaching into my bag with one hand to fumble for my keys while pushing the outer door open with the other. Landon reaches out to hold the door for me and follows me inside the vestibule. In the small space, his proximity is harder to ignore. I find my keys and lift them to the lock on the inner door, but my hand is shaking so badly, I can hardly get them to fit.

He reaches for my hand and takes the keys from me, unlocking the door and gesturing for me to go in. I step into the lobby, tensing when he follows me.

"I'm not going anywhere," he tells me, his voice soft. "Not until you stop lying to me."

I snatch the keys from his hand. "I don't know what you want to hear," I say sharply, leaving him and heading for the stairs. He follows me, and I'm all too aware of him behind me, his eyes on me as I climb the stairs, making my legs feel rubbery. At the door to my apartment, I stop. My emotions are warring inside me. One side is screaming for me to admit my feelings to him, another side is angry with him and with myself for not being stronger. Then there's the sensible part of my brain that's trying to persuade me to stay on course, to stay away from him and protect myself.

I turn around. Landon is at the top step, and he continues to advance until he's only a few strides from me. My eyes fix on his chest, and I search for something to say. "I got your flowers," I offer finally, in a vain attempt to relieve the tension I'm feeling.

He cocks his head, probably surprised by the topic I've chosen. "Did you like them?"

I look up at him and nod silently.

"I liked the article," he says.

"I'm glad." My voice sounds faint, and why do I suddenly feel like crying?

His eyes linger on my lips again, only for a moment, but warmth floods into the lower part of my belly. The urge to walk into his arms and forget everything else is so strong, it takes all my strength to overcome it.

I suck in a breath. "Landon..." I start. I want to tell him it's not a good idea for him to be here, that there's nothing else to say, but he's already moved one step forward, his hand going to the small of my back to pull me the rest of the way toward him. He molds my body to his, lowering his lips to capture mine in a deep, searing kiss.

God! He is possessive, masterful, and so sexy. His lips slide over mine while his tongue probes the seam of my lips, urging me to open my mouth to him. I'm unable...unwilling to resist. He slides his tongue into my mouth to tease and taste mine, and I lose any ability to think. My stomach tightens with need so intense, it's almost painful. I moan softly and he groans in response, the sound vibrating through my body as sweet desire pulses between my legs.

With the hand at my back, he presses my body closer to his while he explores my mouth hungrily. My breasts are crushed against his chest, and my whole body feels weak and hot, melting into his, suffused with craving for him. I kiss him back, hungry for more of the taste of his lips, desperate for his touch.

I thread my fingers through his hair, my whole being reveling in the hunger I can feel coming from him, in the hard ridge of his arousal I can feel pressed against my stomach. I grind against him as the pulsing between my legs intensifies. I want him so much. I want him inside me.

Still kissing me, Landon moves his right hand to cup the curve of my butt while bracing his weight on the door with the other. I want to tear off my clothes, to give him access to the most heated parts of my body. I moan against his mouth, sucking hungrily on his tongue. His answering groan is like a spark in my blood. Any minute now, I'm going to let him fuck me against the door to my apartment, regardless of the fact that anybody could walk up or down the stairs. I want him so damn much.

But I shouldn't.

The thought slips into my mind, the first sensible one I've had since he touched me.

I tear my mouth away from his with a desperate moan, pushing as far back from him as the small space allows. I'm breathing heavily and so is he. His eyes are burning hot with arousal, his pupils dilated, his body so tense I can almost feel the effort it's taking for him to control himself.

"You should leave," I manage. My voice is hoarse, and my hands are shaking. I clench my fingers tightly, trying not to think about the fact that just a few seconds ago, they were buried in his hair. "Please leave."

"Why?" He sounds as confused as I feel. "Rachel, you want this."

I shake my head, my trembling body making the gesture a blatant lie. Every single inch of me is pulsing with unfulfilled desire. I want him to kiss me again. I want him to leave me alone so I can get over him. I don't know what I want.

"Rachel." Landon's voice is firm and patient, urging me to listen. I shake my head stubbornly, but he doesn't stop. "I want you," he says insistently, "and I know you want me. I'm not going to walk away from this."

I want you.

The words send a tremor down my spine, and it takes all my willpower to ignore the feelings they invoke in me. But, we've been here before, and I already know how it ends—me, back in his bed, wondering how long it will last and worried that it won't.

When I don't say anything, he sighs. "Just tell me what you want from me, Rachel."

I want you to love me! The words hover at the tip of my tongue, but I don't say them. Instead, I shake my head. "You keep saying you want me, Landon—for what exactly? Just sex? Indefinitely?"

"This means a lot more than sex and you know it." He touches a finger to my cheek and I start to tremble again. "As long as we both want each other this much, why does it have to end?"

"I don't want you," I tell him stubbornly.

"I already said I won't go anywhere until you stop lying to me." He pushes back from the door and runs a frustrated hand through his hair. "Rachel, this thing we have…"

I inhale sharply. "Landon, I don't want a 'thing'. I don't."

He considers me for a long moment. "So you want something more serious? Some sort of commitment? A relationship?" His eyes flutter closed then open again. "Rachel, that's fine. We can have that if it's what you want, but it's crazy to keep thinking of excuses why we shouldn't be together."

I want to hope, but how different is a 'relationship' from what we've already had? There's still no guarantee that he'll ever allow himself to love me. "A relationship?" I ask softly, folding my arms across my chest. "And that's all?"

He looks at me, brows raised. "What else is there?"

Love…why can't I say the word? Instead, I hold his gaze. "You're willing to let me be a small part of your life, to go out with you once in a while and be seen with you. That's what you call a relationship, isn't it? Then when you've had enough of the sex—which is what this is really all about—that will be the end, won't it?

He throws up his hands. "God! I don't understand you. What the fuck do you want?"

Love. At least a chance at it.

But his thoughts can't even go there. That's how alien the idea of love is to him.

"I can't do this," I whisper. I want to cry. This whole thing with him is so heartbreaking. "I can't... Just go away, Landon. Just leave me alone."

He looks like he's going to say something else, but then he turns and stalks down the stairs, taking them two at a time. I watch him until he disappears, my heart feeling raw, then I take a deep breath, unlock the door, and walk into the apartment.

CHAPTER 4

*W*HEN I close the door behind me, I'm still trembling. Laurie is lying on the couch, her hair piled atop her head, glasses on. She has earbuds stuck in her ear, and her face is deep in one of her gigantic law books. She sees me and rises to a sitting position, taking off her glasses and earbuds.

"So, how was the date with the Jacksshole?" She does a small grimace as she says her version of Jack's name. Obviously, she's still mad at me for 'sabotaging' my relationship with Landon.

"Whatever Laurie," I say tiredly. "I'm going to bed."

She springs up from the couch, looking apologetic. "Rach...I'm sorry about the things I said yester-

63

day." She pauses. "You came in crying, obviously distressed. I should have been supportive instead of blaming you."

"Yeah, you should have," I reply, not ready to be mollified.

She makes a contrite face. "I'm sorry."

"Well, at least you did good right up to the moment I mentioned Jack."

She gives me another small grimace. "I may not understand why you agreed to go out with him, and for the record, I will never understand or support Jack's continued presence in your life." She sighs. "But, I understand how hard it must have been to have no clue where you stand with Landon."

I draw in a breath, willing myself to forget Landon, and how my body reacted to him only a few moments ago. "How are you doing?" I ask Laurie.

She shrugs and drops back on the couch. "Trying to stop refreshing Brett's Facebook page. We're still in a relationship, it seems."

"Have you spoken to him?"

"A few times." A pained frown flits across her face. "He asks how I am, I say I'm fine. Long awkward silence. Then bye-bye."

My shoulders drop. Momentarily forgetting my own heartache, I join her on the couch. "You think you guys will work it out?"

She is silent for a moment. "I don't know," she says finally, shaking her head. "What about Landon? Is it really over with him?"

I nod, filled more with the hope that I can let him go than with any kind of certainty.

Laurie sighs. "What are you going to do?"

"I'll just have to forget about him."

She laughs humorlessly. "If only it was as easy as saying it."

I get up, my mind going back to just a few minutes ago when my body succumbed so easily to Landon's touch. "I'll just have to try."

"Hmm."

"I'm going to bed."

"Okay." She puts her glasses back on and gives me a small smile. "Night night."

THE NEXT MORNING, MARK WILLIS DUMPS AN article from one of our celebrity writers on my desk. I spend the morning reading about her two-week stay in a three-hundred-year-old St Petersburg palace owned by some Russian billionaire and making notes for Mark.

Thankfully, it's engrossing. I read about the ill-fated noble dynasty that once lived there, their beautiful gardens, paintings, and furniture, and somehow, I succeed in pushing thoughts of last night to the back of my mind.

I'm just about done when my phone rings. I frown at Brett's name on the screen. I haven't seen him or spoken with him since the night he told Laurie they needed some time apart.

"Brett." I try to keep the edge out of my voice, but I'm still pissed at him and it shows.

"Hi." He releases a breath with the word, like he's relieved I picked up. "How're you?"

"I'm okay."

I hear him sigh. There's none of the usual playfulness in his voice. In fact, he sounds as dejected as I know Laurie feels. "And Laurie? How's she?"

"You know you could call her and ask her yourself," I say with a small snort.

He is quiet. "Can we meet, for lunch or something?"

I frown. "Today?"

"If you have the time. I'd really like to talk to you."

There's a hint of a plea in his voice. I sigh and look at my watch—it's almost noon. "Yeah, I guess."

"Great." He sounds genuinely glad. We decide to meet at a deli close to my office, and he's already waiting when I get there. He's seated at a table close to the window, restlessly tapping his fingers on the surface. His t-shirt has the logo of his gym printed on the front, and his curly black hair flops endearingly over his forehead and ears. He's always been fit, especially since he started the gym, but now he looks like he's lost some weight, and not in a good way.

I slide into the seat opposite him. "You look awful," I tell him, feeling a little sympathy.

"I know," he replies with a long, tired sigh.

An impatient waitress comes around to take my sandwich order. Brett orders the same thing, grilled chicken and vegetable with a large mixed fruit smoothie. When she leaves, Brett leans forward. "It's not that I haven't asked Laurie. I have."

"She told me," I say with a shamefaced look. "I was just being a bitch earlier."

He sighs. "I deserve it, don't I?"

"Yeah kinda."

He is quiet. The waitress returns with our drinks and this time, she pauses to smile at Brett and ask him if he needs anything else.

I notice that he hardly looks at her when he says no. "What do you think?" he asks me. "How is she really?"

I sigh. "What do you want, Brett? Do you want to be with Laurie or not?"

"You know I do." He closes his eyes then leans

back in his chair, and I see the pain etched on his face. "Did she ever mention... Do you think she wants to break up?"

I shake my head. "Now or before?"

"Before." He pauses. "Now too. Does she want to end things?"

"No," I reassure him. "She never mentioned anything like that to me."

The waitress brings our food, sullen and impatient again. I wait for her to leave before biting into the sandwich.

"Good?" Brett asks.

I nod.

He sips from his smoothie, ignoring the sandwich on his plate. There's a small frown on his face, and I can tell he's deep in thought.

"Hey," I say softly. "Come on, eat something."

He smiles and picks up his sandwich. We eat silently, but it's clear he has a lot on his mind.

"We've been fighting a lot," he says once we're done eating. "One minute it's all good, and the next, I'm walking home, miserable as hell."

I keep silent, not sure what to say to that...some useless platitude like *everybody fights*?

"When she makes a big deal about the little things," Brett continues, "I just feel like maybe she really wants me gone. We've been together for four years, Rach. It's scary. I know I want to spend the rest of my life with her. I know I love her more than anything in the world, but what if deep down she feels trapped and it's my fault?"

I've never seen anything to make me think Laurie feels trapped, and I rush to reassure him of that. "I can bet she doesn't feel that way, Brett." I sigh. "Why not tell her how you really feel? Your fears and everything. You love each other, you can work through it."

He nods gratefully. "You're right, I will. I'll talk to her."

I smile, but deep inside, I feel like a hypocrite. I haven't been able to apply the same principle in my life. I haven't been able to tell Landon how I feel, but here I am doling out advice.

We say goodbye outside the deli, and I wade through the lunch hour body traffic toward my office, truly hoping that Laurie and Brett would work it out so things can go back to the way they were.

At least the way they were before I met Landon.

I want you, and I'm not going to walk away from this.

My mind fills with images of last night and need courses through me. I struggle against the memories, pushing into the Gilt lobby and practically bumping into Jack.

"Whoa." He holds out a hand to steady me, and somehow I end up pressed against his body in the most awkward hug ever. It's clear he doesn't feel that way about it, as there's a teasing grin on his face. "What's the hurry, beautiful?"

"Nothing." I return his smile, stepping back so he has to let me go. My face is still flushed from all the carnal images of Landon that were rolling through my mind only moments ago. "Just escaping my demons."

Jack arches a brow. "Your rich, handsome prince not slaying them for you?"

I ignore the dig—my 'prince' is the demon I'm trying to escape anyway. "I gotta get to work."

"Hey." He sounds conciliatory. "Last night was great. It was good to catch up."

I give him a small smile. "Yea."

"So..." There's a hopeful look on his face. "Still coming tonight?"

To see his mother. I nod. "I already said yes. Just tell me when."

"Whenever you get off work." He pauses. "I really appreciate this. It means a lot."

Don't let it mean too much, I start to say, but I shrug and let it go. "It's no bother, really." Every moment I spend busy with something, anything at all, is a moment I don't think about Landon.

I get off work later than usual, and Jack is waiting for me at the reception desk on our floor when I finally leave the office. We take the elevator down together, sharing it with a group of interns who can't stop looking at him. In the ground floor lobby, Chelsea is having a conversation with one of the downstairs receptionists. She sees me with Jack and her eyes widen. "What. The. Hell," she mouths slowly.

I shrug, and she wags a finger at me.

Outside, Jack hails a cab. During the short journey, he's mostly silent, and I assume he's nervous.

His mother has an apartment in Gramercy Park. The doorman eyes Jack suspiciously while checking his name on the visitor's list then directs us to the elevator, which soon deposits us in a thickly carpeted vestibule. There are four doors with gold-lettered apartment numbers, and one of them opens just as we exit the elevator. The woman in the doorway is petite, her black hair held up in a ballet bun, which brings the elegant angles of her face into focus. Her eyes are gray like Jack's, and very sharp. She's dressed all in black, the only color a hint of red lipstick.

Her eyes lose their sharpness as they settle eagerly on Jack, roaming from his hair to his shoes, almost as if she needs to reassure herself that he's really there. Then she lets out a breath and her glance flicks toward me.

"I see you brought a buffer," she says with a small chuckle.

SERENA GREY

"Hello Mother." I'm surprised at how subdued Jack sounds.

She ignores him. "Who are you?"

"Rachel Foster," Jack says before I can respond. "We work together at Gilt. Rachel, my mother, Gertrude Weyland."

"I'm an admirer of your work," I say sincerely.

She snorts, unimpressed. "When you're my age, you won't be very flattered that the 'work' everyone loves is something you wrote in your early twenties when you were young and foolish."

I don't know what to say to that, so I stay silent. She disappears from the doorway. I hear her voice inside the apartment, telling someone, "My son is here." I follow Jack inside. The large living room is stark, which is to be expected since she lives abroad. There are only a few pieces of furniture, but the ceilings are high and vaulted, and a few walls are covered with modern art. I even recognize one of my mother's paintings hanging on a far wall.

She drops gracefully onto a white leather couch, where an older guy with beautiful silver hair and intelligent green eyes is already seated.

"So you're Jack," he says, getting up to shake Jack's hand.

"I have no idea who you are," Jack says churlishly, ignoring the hand extended toward him.

72

"I'm Curtis James," the man tries again.

"Well, you have nice hair. Maybe you'll last longer than the others."

I've never seen Jack act so childish, and it would be funny if I weren't so shocked. Curtis gives up and puts his hand back in his pocket. As he goes back to his seat, I catch a small smile flit across Gertrude's face.

"Curtis is my dermatologist." She directs her reply to me. "He's been showing me wonderful ways to keep my skin looking young." Her lips lift in a small, naughty smile, and Jack snorts, muttering something under his breath. She ignores him. "Why don't you sit, Rachel? You too Jack."

"Thank you." I choose one of the single armchairs. Curtis is smiling at me, and I smile back.

"You're not exotic in any way. You're not a model." Gertrude is peering at me. "You're nothing like any of the girls the gossip magazines like to link with my son. What's your appeal?"

"Mother..."

"Like you said, I'm only the buffer," I reply pleasantly, wondering inside if I just willingly walked into the definition of dysfunctional.

"I did say that." She arches her brow at me. "So you work at Gilt?"

"Yes, Gilt Traveler."

She nods. A man comes in with drinks on a tray—four large black tumblers with green veggie straws sticking out of them.

Gertrude sighs. "I don't do dinner anymore. I hope you don't mind smoothies. They're very healthy."

We each take a tumbler, and the man disappears. Jack glares at his glass like he'd rather die than taste the contents.

"So, you're a travel writer?" Curtis asks.

"I write for a travel magazine."

"I've never liked travel writing," Gertrude says. "Anybody can write about climbing mountains and jumping out of airplanes." She gives Jack a meaningful look. "Real fiction demands imagination."

"I'm sorry I didn't inherit your imagination gene," he mutters.

"You've tried very hard to make up for it. I labored for fourteen hours to bring your body into the world, but every time I open your magazine or take a look at those damn TV shows, I have to watch you throw that body around and risk breaking it into pieces." Her voice doesn't rise as she says this, but I watch Jack retreat into himself. He looks miserable, and it's hard not to pity him.

"Jack's a brilliant writer," I say, facing Gertrude.

She sighs. "We're saying the same thing."

There's a short awkward silence.

"I subscribe to the Gilt Review," Curtis says. "The short stories are brilliant."

"You think so?" Gertrude is smiling, like she knows a secret. She looks at me. "Do you read it?"

I nod. "Every issue." I initially applied to work at the Review and ended up as an assistant at Traveler. I still hoped to one day make the move to the Gilt Review.

"What do you think about it?" She leans forward, her eyes bright, like she really needs to know my opinion. At that moment, I see the similarity with her son; they both possess the charm that can make their audience forget everything else.

"I think it's fair to call it the modern voice of literature. However, I'd include less work from established authors and more from unknown, fledgling writers. After all, it's the job of a magazine like the Gilt Review to widen the reader's scope."

Gertrude considers me for a moment, still smiling. "That's an informed opinion," she observes.

"Rachel always wanted to work at the Review," Jack offers. "She applied there, but they sent her to us."

"Is that right?" His mother smiles at me. "Why don't you apply again?" She gives me an encouraging smile and I'm reminded of Jessica Layner, my boss.

"You might be surprised." She pauses. "You haven't touched your drink," she observes.

I steel myself and take a sip. It's surprisingly delicious. "What's in this?"

"Fruits and vegetables." She grins, and it's exactly the same as Jack's grin. "I'll bet you thought it'd be awful."

"I did," I confess.

"Not everything about me is awful," she says. "My relationships with the men in my life, maybe." She looks at Jack. "Stop sulking, dear. Tell us about your work. I'm sure you haven't outgrown talking about yourself."

Jack braves a bit of the smoothie then with a pained expression in his mother's direction, he starts to tell us about his trip to South America and falling ill. Gertrude listens intently as he tries to impress her with his narration and his experiences. She asks questions about his safety, health risks he took, places he stayed. She's genuinely worried about him, regardless of how unimpressed she is with what he does. He, on the other hand, wants her to appreciate his work while being very unconcerned about his own personal safety.

The conversation continues in the same vein for the rest of the night. By the time we're ready to leave, I feel a bit sorry for Jack. He's silent all the way downstairs. The doorman asks if we need a cab, but Jack shakes his head.

"I think I'm going to walk for a little while," he tells me.

I shrug. "All right."

We start along the sidewalk. "I'm sorry about..." Jack searches for the words. "All that. It's just hard to be in the same room with her."

"I thought she had a weird kind of charm," I say gently. "Of course it's different when it's your relative." I pause. "Are you okay?"

"I'm angry." He sighs. "All my life I've never seen her for more than a month every year, but every single hour I'm with her she makes me feel like my choices are shit."

"Your choices aren't shit," I assure him. "You're really talented as a writer, and people love your TV shows."

He stops walking. "You really think I'm talented?"

"Yes, and so does your mom, by the way."

He snorts. "But no one can compete with Gertrude Weyland, author of the great American novel." There is a heavy bitterness in his tone.

"What about your dad?"

He stops walking. "I don't know who he is. She never told me. Probably some poor sucker like Curtis whatshisname who fell for her 'weird' charm." He frowns and looks up and down the street for a cab. "I'd better get you home. Thanks for being here with me tonight."

"I'm glad I was," I say with a smile.

Maybe it's because I feel so sorry for him, but I don't stop him when he moves toward me. I ready myself for a hug, but I'm shocked when he places his hands on my shoulders and leans in to kiss me.

Confusion keeps me frozen, but only for a moment. I push at his chest, freeing myself from the coming contact. "Stop it," I mutter. "For God's sake Jack. I thought we were past this."

"You thought...?" He shakes his head. "Look, I know you think the worst of me right now because of what happened two years ago, and that night at the Swanson Court when you found out I'd gotten engaged—"

"Jack, I don't care about that anymore."

"But I do." He sighs. "It was different with you. It always was, and I wanted to be the kind of man you deserved, and I tried, for two months, but I knew I was only going to hurt you. You've seen my mother. She never kept a man around for more than a few months, and that's the example I had."

I shake my head. "Stop it."

"No." There is a storm of entreaty in his eyes. "I didn't want you to love me because I thought you deserved better. I was a fool, and I know you've held that against me all this time."

I shake my head. "Not anymore. I told you, I've let it go."

"What if I don't want you to? What if..." He trails off. "You *have* to remember how good we were together." His eyes are imploring. "I know I messed everything up, but it's not too late. A few weeks ago, you still cared about me. That day at the Swanson Court, you said that being with me was the best thing that ever happened to you...that can't have changed."

"It has." I hold his gaze. "Jack, I fell in love with someone else."

His face hardens. "Landon Court doesn't deserve you."

"And you do?" I snort. "Don't make me laugh."

He looks crushed. "Okay, maybe I don't deserve you, but I'm not blind. These past few days you've been a shadow of yourself. I know about him, Rachel. He's heartless with women. He'll use you and then he'll toss you aside. He has hurt you already, hasn't he? I know you. I can fucking see it in your face."

I close my eyes. "You're only seeing what you want to see."

"Am I?" He laughs bitterly. "So where is he, this perfect Landon Court? Why are you here with me if you're so fucking happy with him?"

If I were a different sort of person, I'd hit him. I want to, very badly, but I clench my fists and grit my teeth. "I'm sorry I listened when you begged me to come with you to see your mother. Clearly, I should have ignored you."

"Rachel..." He steps toward me and I hold up one hand to stop him.

"Why am I suddenly so important to you, Jack? Because there's another man in the picture? Someone who maybe makes you feel insecure?" I watch as his eyes narrow slightly, but I continue, anger and regret for all the months I wasted on him making me emotional. "Tell me, if I'd never met Landon, if I'd still been waiting on the sidelines, hoping you'd see past your bevy of models and athletes and exotic beauties to notice me, I'd still be right there, wouldn't I? The only reason you suddenly can't let me go is that I don't want you anymore."

He starts to say something else, but I notice a cab coming down the street and hail it. Luckily, it's empty and quickly comes to a stop in front of us. Just before I climb in, I give Jack one more glance. He's watching me, his eyes clouded, his hands shoved into his pockets.

"Goodbye Jack," I say quietly.

He doesn't reply.

CHAPTER 5

*L*ANDON *Court doesn't deserve you.*

If it weren't so frustrating, it would be funny how everything always came back to Landon. Even an evening with Jack had somehow managed to devolve into an emotional conversation about Landon.

He'll use you and then he'll toss you aside.

It's not as if I didn't know that already. I've spent the past few days pushing Landon away just to protect myself from that imminent hurt, but no matter how hard I try, there he is, in my head, and physically too, refusing to let me go.

I sigh, pushing all my thoughts about Landon, about Jack and his ill-timed realization that we had something 'good' to the deepest darkest recesses of my mind. There, at least, they won't threaten to drive me insane.

I decide to call my mom, because it's been a few days, and for some reason, I find myself appreciating her more. She answers on the fourth ring. "Sweetheart," she coos in her low, smooth voice, and I sigh, feeling homesick.

"Hi Mom."

"How are you? I hope there's nothing wrong."

I'm tempted to break down and tell her how miserable I am. I hold back, but just barely.

"No, nothing's wrong. I'm good. Laurie's good."

"You're fine," she corrects then laughs. "I'm glad you're both okay." There's a pause. "Your father and I will be in the city on Thursday. I have an art thing."

It's always an 'art' thing with my mom. Even showing her work in a prestigious gallery is 'an art thing'. I still don't know if she's so blasé because of how successful she is, or because she really doesn't care about events.

I'm in front of my building by now, and I step out of the cab. "Will I see you guys?"

"If you want," she replies. "You could come with. We'll pick you up on our way. Laurie too. It's a black-tie thing at the Remington House."

"The…what house now?"

She sighs, probably exasperated by my ignorance.

"The Remington House is a historic mansion on Fifth," she informs me. When I don't say anything in reply, she continues her lecture. "Shelby Remington, the last living member of the Remington family, left the house and his entire art collection to the Remington Trust. It's a museum now. Two Cornelia Eames paintings he lost in a bet a long time ago are being restored to the house. I'm giving a speech."

At least I know the name of the artist. I've paid enough attention to my mother's work over the years to recognize the name of one of the impressionists whose work she studied in college. Cornelia Eames contributed much more than paintings to art. The trust she established still sends aspiring artists to art schools in Europe every year.

"I'll ask Laurie," I say, letting myself into the apartment. The lights are off, which means Laurie isn't home yet.

"She needs a night out," my mom remarks. "There's no benefit in staying home inside your brain when you're miserable about a man. She needs to dress up, look beautiful, go out, and maybe flirt a little. It works every time."

This is why I can't tell my mom how broken up I am about Landon—she probably won't let me rest until she prescribes a remedy to help me find a way out of my heartbreak.

"I'll let her know."

"Hmm." There's a pause at her end. "I read your article. Good work there, sweetheart. Your dad thinks so too."

"Thanks," I say bleakly. What had made me think I could have any conversation, with anyone, without having to talk about Landon and the damned article about his hotel?

It gets worse. "So...how are things with Landon?"

I close my eyes, dreading the answer I have to give. "We're not seeing each other anymore."

"Oh!" I can hear the surprise in her voice, and I don't blame her. Just a few days ago, Landon was charming his way through my family. "How are you?"

I try to keep it light. "I'll survive."

"He seemed so into you," she muses. "I was so sure..." She trails off. "Are you okay? Really?"

"Of course," I say brightly, resisting the urge to tell her everything. "I'm just, you know, trying my best not to think about it."

She sighs. "Well, I'll see you tomorrow night. I love you, sweetheart, and give Laurie a kiss for me."

After the call, I change into my nightwear and settle in bed with a book about writing style. I plan to read until I fall asleep, and hopefully be too tired to dwell on Landon. I'm a few minutes into the book when Laurie arrives. She comes straight into my room and drops onto the bed beside me, still wearing her clothes from the office.

"Rough day?"

She sighs. "They're all rough these days." She stares at the cover of my book for a minute. "I had dinner with Brett."

I allow myself to hope, even though her demeanor doesn't point to an ecstatic reunion. "So, what happened?"

"He told me he saw you at lunch." She looks at me. "What did he say?"

I shrug. "That he loves you." I look at her. "And he really does." She looks away and I continue. "He's miserable when you guys fight, and he's afraid that because you guys have been together for so long, you might have a subliminal desire to break up, which is why you pick fights with him."

"That's the part that pisses me off," Laurie declares, rising from the bed. "He told me the same thing. How can he think that in my subconscious or wherever, I really want to leave him? Like I don't know my own freaking mind?"

Her temper is getting the best of her. "Laurie, he's just telling you how he feels."

"But why should he feel like that?" She frowns. "I don't fight about 'little' things. Letting a co-worker at the gym flirt with him is not a 'little' thing. It's a big deal to me."

I drop my book. "Maybe make him understand? Tell him how it makes you feel?"

She sniffs and buries her face in her hands. "I'm tired of fighting," she says softly.

Me too. I'm sick of fighting all the feelings tearing me up inside. I wish there was a way to escape, to forget. I sigh, remembering the conversation with my mom. "How do you feel about a black-tie cocktail art thing on Thursday?"

"Your mom?"

I nod.

"Where?"

"Some historic mansion. They'll pick us up." I grin. "So now we can worry about what to wear and not think about men for tonight at least."

She looks grateful. "That seriously sounds great."

WE STAY UP LATE, CONSIDERING AND DISMISSING clothes from our wardrobes, and for a while I manage to forget the numbness inside. We end up going to bed around midnight after finally deciding on which dresses, shoes, and jewelry to wear, and in the morning, we both have to rush to make it out early.

By the time I'm done with the morning meetings with the other members of the writing team and an intense editing session with Mark, I start to think that maybe it's time to congratulate myself. I've actually managed to go through the whole morning without tormenting myself about Landon. Maybe it's because I've been really busy, but it gives me hope that I can get over him, that maybe with time, I'll stop thinking about him at all.

I'm still having those thoughts when the package arrives late in the afternoon. It's a delivery from the Swanson Court International, and the sender is Tony Gillies, Landon's assistant. Inside is a gilt-edged envelope containing a full-access invitation to the grand reopening of the Gold Dust Hotel.

I stare at the back of the invite, at the image of the hotel embossed in gold leaf on the smooth velvety stationery. I close my eyes, suddenly weak with yearning. All of a sudden, my mind is flooded with the memories of that week in San Francisco, when it was just me and Landon, when I slowly and completely fell in love with him.

I'm not going to walk away from this.

But I am, and I have. Why is it so hard for him to understand and accept that I want to move on? Why can't he just leave me alone?

Why does everything have to be about what he

wants? What about me? I want a chance to get over him, to move on with my life.

I pick up my phone without thinking and dial his number. I wait as the phone rings, my anger slowly plateauing when he doesn't pick up.

Almost relieved, I place my phone on my desk. I'm probably overreacting, I decide. Maybe the invitation isn't a big deal. It makes sense for me to be at the opening; I wrote an article about the hotel, after all.

I start as the sound of my ringtone breaks into my thoughts. Landon's name is flashing on the screen. I hesitate for a moment, not sure anymore that I want to talk to him, but finally I pick up the phone and accept the call.

"Hello."

"Rachel."

There's something about the way he says my name...it makes me weak and emotional. I swallow, suddenly at a loss for what to say. Now I can't remember exactly what I was angry about.

"Rachel," Landon says again. His voice is cool and controlled, a far contrast to the turmoil I'm feeling. How can he be like that when I feel like I'm being torn apart?

"I received a delivery of an invitation to the opening of the Gold Dust," I say, keeping my voice as aloof as I can manage. "I'm assuming it's a mistake."

His deep chuckle is followed by a short silence. *I shouldn't have called*, I realize suddenly. I could have ignored the package, but I wanted any excuse to talk to him, to hear his voice. I sigh inwardly. He probably knows.

"Why would you assume that?" he asks finally.

I swallow. "Because there's no reason for me to be there?"

"I want you there," he says, "with me."

There's no doubt in his voice, and the confidence, the certainty...it does things to my insides. "Why?" I ask, my voice low.

"Do I have to tell you?" I hear him sigh. "I want you by my side, and not just at the opening. In fact, forget the invite, Rachel. Just tell me what I have to do, let me know what you want from me."

I try not to imagine being at his side while he opens his beautiful new hotel. I try not to fall in love with the image of us together. I try not to want it desperately.

"I don't want anything from you," I say softly.

"You're lying," he says. "I can hear it in your voice."

"No. I'm not." I steel myself. "It's over Landon. It should have been over the moment I left your apartment that first night." I sigh. "You should never have tried to find me, and I should never have accepted your ridiculous proposal. That's the truth. What did you think, that you'd ask me to fly across the country with you and suddenly I'd forget..." I trail off.

"Forget what?"

I'm quiet. *That I can't be with you. That I can't keep on being in love with you.* "That I've moved on, because I have moved on, Landon—and you should too."

He doesn't reply. "I have a meeting," he says after a long pause. "We'll finish this conversation later."

He's gone before I can respond.

THERE'S NO CONVERSATION TO FINISH. THERE'S nothing else to talk about. By evening, I'm still on edge. My phone is like a bomb about to go off any moment as I wait for Landon to call me back. What did he mean about finishing the conversation? The conversation was already completed.

When my phone rings just as I'm getting ready to go home, my heart jumps, but it's only Laurie.

"Hello," I breathe, my voice weak with a mixture of relief and disappointment.

"Hey," she says. "You ready to leave?"

"Just about." I frown. "Why?"

"I'm downstairs in the lobby," she informs me. "I decided to walk, and I thought you might like to join me. So, you need some company for the long walk home? I know I do."

"I'll be right down," I tell her, gathering my things.

In reception on my floor, there's a familiar figure stepping into the elevator in front of me. "Hold the elevator," I call out at the same moment he turns around and I realize it's Chadwick.

"Chadwick!"

He grins, putting a hand out to stop the doors. He looks great, his long brown hair drawn into a bun at the back of his head, like some hot new-age guru. His sweet caramel eyes are soft and smiling. "It sounds like you're happy to see me."

I join him in the elevator and grab him in a tight hug. My relationship with Chadwick is uncomplicated. I know he'd like to sleep with me, and he takes my refusal to fall into bed with him with good humor. It's refreshing, with no pressure whatsoever. "I'm always happy to see you, Chad."

He gives me a sidelong glance. "So...not that I have anything against elevators, but...can I suggest we go somewhere more private so you can show me how happy you really are?"

I giggle and swat him on the shoulder. "How are you?"

"Still hot for you." He winks. "How are you?"

"Hanging there."

"You ran off," he says accusingly. "That night at my party, you disappeared almost as soon as you arrived."

The memories of that night at the Swanson Court come crashing into my head. Landon...always Landon. I sigh. "I'm sorry, Chad. I had... Something came up and I had to leave."

He accepts my excuse with a nod just as the doors swish open and we walk out into the ground floor lobby. Laurie is standing by the self-opening glass doors at the entrance, and she waves as soon as she sees me. I wave back, and Chadwick's eyes follow the direction, landing on Laurie.

He does a quick double take. "Wow."

I don't blame him. Laurie is gorgeous even on the most ordinary days. Right now in her slim-fitting pants and stylish pink blouse with her hair falling down to her back in soft black waves, she looks exceptional. I give Chadwick a warning look. "Don't even think about it. She's my cousin."

"What an incredible gene pool," he exclaims softly, following me toward the entrance. Laurie gives him an appreciative onceover before turning to me. "You ready?"

"Yeah." Chadwick is still standing beside me, staring at her, his jaw somewhere on the floor. "Er... this is Chadwick," I say, somewhat amused. "Chadwick Black. Chad, my cousin Laurie."

"*The* Chadwick Black?" Laurie eyes him from head to toe. "Hi." She draws out the word.

For the first time since I've known him, Chadwick looks as if he doesn't know what to say. "You're absolutely beautiful," he says finally.

"I know," Laurie replies with a laugh.

"Of course you do." He still looks gobsmacked. "I want to take pictures of you."

She gives him a small, amused frown. "No."

"I probably want to marry you."

"Ha ha." Laurie grins. "Nope."

He puts a hand on his chest. "My heart is broken."

"He's cute," Laurie tells me, laughing. She turns back to Chadwick. "Rachel's told me so much about your work."

Chadwick grins, recovering himself a little. "Only my work?"

Laurie laughs again, looking up into his face and touching him lightly on the shoulder. She's flirting. "It was nice to meet you, Chadwick," she tells him before linking her arm through mine as we leave the building.

"He is hot," she says once we're out of earshot.

"He's a slut."

Laurie snorts. "Aren't they all?"

I don't have anything to say to that. As we walk along the sidewalk, Laurie pulls out two candy bars from her bag and offers me one. I bite into the chewy sweetness and sigh, wondering how many I'd have to eat in order to forget my craving for Landon.

"I've got more in my bag," Laurie announces, almost as if she can read my thoughts.

I grin. "If I ever become obese, you'll have yourself to blame."

"I'll be right there obese with you." She laughs. "At least if we're fat and unattractive, we won't have to worry about men."

"It'll make a good reality show," I quip. "Fat Fosters or something."

We're still laughing when a couple walks out of a deli a few feet in front of us.

Laurie stops laughing first, because she sees them before I do. They step out at the same time, the guy holding the door open for the girl. When the door closes behind them, she puts her arms around him in a heartfelt hug then draws away and squeezes his hand before walking away.

It's a tender moment—at least it would be if the guy wasn't Brett. I look quickly from him to Laurie, and she looks as if she's just been slapped.

When Brett notices us, his eyes fix on Laurie and there's a brief flash of panic on his face. He starts toward us but Laurie pulls at my hand and hurries down the sidewalk, and I have no choice but to follow her.

"Laurie," Brett calls from behind us, but she acts as if she can't hear him.

He catches up in a few steps. "Laurie, wait. It's not what you think."

She spins around to face him. "Don't," she snaps. "Just leave me the fuck alone."

She starts to walk again, and I give Brett an apologetic shrug before following her. She doesn't stop or reduce her pace until we're right in front of our building.

"Are you all right?" I ask when we finally slow down. I'm almost panting from the exertion.

"I should have changed into my walking shoes," she replies, shaking her head. "My feet hurt."

She obviously doesn't want to talk about Brett.

When we get to the apartment, she still hasn't said anything about what we saw. I close the door behind us and watch as she walks toward her room.

"Laurie," I say gently. "You know it could have been nothing."

She stops, her whole body completely still for a long moment before she turns to look at me. Her eyes are full of tears. "Yeah, but it could have been something."

I shake my head. "That's unlikely. He wouldn't... He loves you."

"It's her," she says, her voice cracking. "She's the reason we had this fight in the first place. She came on to him, and now they're having lunch and hugging on the street? Did you see the way she smiled at him, the way she held his hand? Did that look like nothing to you? Like the 'little things' I'm not supposed to fight with him about?" She stops talking and wipes her eyes angrily. "I'm never going to see stuff like that and not feel horrible about it. It's never going to be okay."

She tosses her bag on the couch and goes to sit beside it. I can hear her phone ringing inside the bag, but she ignores it. I know it's probably Brett, and I wish she would let him explain.

Her phone stops ringing, and almost immediately, mine starts. Even before I fish it out of my bag and glance at the screen, I already know who it is. "It's Brett," I tell Laurie gently. "I think he really wants to talk."

She stretches out her hand for the phone, and as soon as I hand it to her she swipes across the screen to reject the call. When she hands the phone back to me, her hands are shaking.

I sigh. "I think I know what we need."

She looks at me, her face tight with the determination not to cry. "What?"

"Ice cream," I suggest. "Lots of it."

There is a small flash of gratitude in her eyes. She sighs. "That might help."

"It had better," I say confidently, going to our tiny kitchen in search of the tub of ice cream we have in the freezer. I come back empty. "We're out," I tell Laurie.

She grins sheepishly. "I could have told you that."

I purse my lips, glad that she's smiling, at least. "I'm going to run downstairs to get some. Don't go anywhere."

She holds up her hands as if to say, *Where would I go?* "I'll be right here."

I COME BACK ARMED WITH ENOUGH ICE CREAM AND wine to start me and Laurie on our journey to becoming obese drunks, and I'm trying to unlock the door when I hear the sound of her laughter. Puzzled,

I enter the apartment, wondering what could have become funny in my absence.

I don't have to wonder for long. Laurie is still sitting on the couch where I left her, but now she's not alone. Landon is sitting on our armchair, smiling at whatever he said that's so amusing.

My first instinct is to turn around and leave, to go somewhere he won't be able to find me, pull me in with his presence, and make me silly with desire.

But why should I be the one to leave? What gives him the right to invade my personal space again and again? And why, for God's sake, did Laurie let him in?

He turns to look at me, still smiling, but as his eyes meet mine, the merriment disappears, replaced by a piercing look that makes my stomach knot tightly.

"Hello, Rachel."

I glare at him, even though every single inch of my skin is already flushed and my body is thrumming with awareness. I'm frustrated and angry, but those feelings are mixed with something else—sadness, desire, longing? I give Laurie an accusing look. "You're obviously feeling better. Maybe I shouldn't have bothered with these."

She rolls her eyes and gets up from the couch. She clearly thinks I'm overreacting, but she has no idea how difficult it's been for me these past few days.

"You're a lifesaver," she says, coming to take the bag from me, all the while looking unapologetic about allowing me to find Landon here without any warning at all.

"What. The. Fuck, Laurie?" I mouth silently.

She gives me a helpless shrug and disappears into the kitchen, leaving me with no choice but to fix my glare on Landon once again.

"What are you doing here?" I'm still standing close to the door. My eyes slide over him, taking in every beloved angle and plane of his face, and the perfect dark gray suit that's almost but not *quite* as sexy as the man wearing it. I want to tear my eyes away, but somehow, I can't. I feel so confused, annoyed, aroused...

He gets up in one fluid, graceful movement, immediately dwarfing the room. "What do you think I'm doing?"

His voice is low, but I feel the words like a threat, to my body and to my peace of mind. Steeling myself, I give him a challenging look. "You need to leave."

He raises a brow. "You have to start saying that like you really mean it," he says. "But we both know you don't."

Laurie returns from the kitchen before I can reply. She's carrying a glass of wine and a bowl of ice cream. She takes in the sight of me and Landon facing each other and gives me a wide-eyed smile. "I'm just gonna…" She jerks her head in the direction of her room. "It was nice to see you again Landon."

"Likewise." He smiles at her, his co-conspirator. My scowl deepens as she disappears into her room and closes the door.

"So you've moved on?"

He's facing me again, and I step back, something in his tone making me want to run. My back hits the door just as his long strides bring him right in front of me.

"Is that why you came here?" I let a mocking note creep into my voice. "You couldn't bear the thought that there's one woman in the whole world who isn't beside herself with joy at the thought that you want a *relationship* with her?"

"Jesus! Rachel." He closes the remaining distance between us, effectively backing me up against the door. With both of his palms flat on either side of me, I'm trapped. He's so close, and I'm so aware, that if he comes any nearer, he'll have his whole body plastered over mine. I'm nervous and excited, but I'm not going to let him seduce me into submission—not again.

His eyes rake my face. What's he looking for, I wonder—signs of capitulation? He lowers his head, and at the thought that he's going to kiss me, my stomach flips and my lips part, my breath suddenly coming hard and fast.

But he doesn't kiss me. "I'm at my wits end," he whispers softly. "I'm helpless, bewitched. You're my every waking thought and sleeping dream." He brings his lips close to my ear and I bite back a moan at the sensation. "You want me," he says, "and I'm going crazy. Stop lying to me. Tell me what I have to do."

My belly is a tight knot of need and frustration. I pull in a breath through my parted lips. "I don't—" I start.

He doesn't let me finish. His lips cover mine, hot, sensual, hungry. All the emotions I'm feeling, all the anger, all the pain transforms into a wild, electric jolt of pleasure that pierces from my lips to my pulsing, needy core.

I tear my lips away from his with a gasp. I'm already panting, and my whole body feels flushed with heat. I wish he'd kiss me again. I wish he'd make me forget all the thoughts warring in my head and just fuck me, hard and fast and sweet.

I wish I could stop thinking about what would happen after that.

"Stop it." I breathe loudly. His face is less than an inch from mine, and his body is pressed against me, warm, hard, and so familiar.

"I can't," he says simply, and the bare admission is

like a knife in my resolve. "You owe me an explanation," he continues. "You're driving me insane trying to understand what the fuck's going on. I acted like a jackass on Sunday. I was jealous. The thought of you spending any time with your ex...it made me unreasonable. I'm sorry."

I don't say anything. I clench my hands into fists, afraid I'm going to cry, or worse, give in to him.

"I need you," he murmurs. His breath warms the skin below my ear, making my skin tingle. A soft sigh escapes my lips. "Stop pushing me away," he continues, and I feel his hand skim the side of my breast. His fingers barely touch me, but my nipples harden, the tight peaks pushing out from under my clothes, begging for more.

His breath comes out in a hard rush, and his lips trail a sweet path along my hairline. Heat pulses between my legs, and through the layers of clothes between us, I can feel his need for me, hard and thick, guaranteed to give me the pleasure I need.

"I want you." His voice is bewitching, mesmerizing...the voice of temptation. "I want all of you, and I'm going crazy with the need to touch you. I want to bury myself so deep inside you, it would be impossible to tell where you end and I begin. I want to hear you scream when you come. I can hardly think of anything else.

My body clenches with raw, insistent need. I can't find enough air to fill my lungs. I close my eyes, the combination of his proximity and the things he's saying making me unable to think of anything but wild, multi-orgasmic sex.

"I remember everything," he whispers in my ear. "The sounds you make in your throat, the exquisite taste of your pussy, the way you cry out when you come, the perfect curve of your breast in my hand." He looks into my face, his eyes heated and imploring. "I remember what it's like to sleep with you in my arms, Rachel, and sometimes I don't know what I want more—to fuck you or just to hold you.

I feel like if he keeps talking, I might just come from the sound of his voice in my ear. "Please," I whisper. I don't know what I'm begging for. I don't know if I want him to do everything my body is screaming for, or if I want him to leave.

"Please...what?" One hand moves to my waist, his fingers flexing at my back. I gasp as the pulse of arousal and heat intensifies between my legs.

I look helplessly into his face. "Please," I croak. "Please leave."

His eyes close, and he straightens, taking a step back. He turns his face away when he opens his eyes, concentrating on the windows for a few moments.

When he looks back at me, his expression is one of resignation.

I clench my fists, resisting the desperate urge to surrender myself to him. We're both silent, and I'm almost afraid to move. He gestures toward the door at my back, and I slowly step away from it, watching him, feeling a profound loss, as well as excruciating, devastating pain.

"I'm..." He sighs. "God!" He smiles then, and it's a humorless smile. "I'm sorry," he says bitterly.

Then he's gone, the door closing with a soft click behind him. Immediately I burst into tears, unable to hold it in anymore. The sobs wrack my body as I slide down onto the floor, wondering why everything has to be so fucking difficult.

CHAPTER 6

"$\mathcal{I}$N fifty years, this building will no longer be here," my mom declares. "There'll be some ugly glass monolith instead."

"You don't know that," my dad replies. He's looking distinguished in a black tux. My mom, in a burgundy evening gown with her hair in a stylish chignon, looks elegant. I really think she could pass for my sister if she tried. We're in the old ballroom of the Remington House. It's a lovely place, decorated in the beaux-arts style with high ceilings, arched windows, ornamental wall carvings, and patterned marble floors. There are paintings from different eras hanging on the walls, all part of the Remington collection. In the front of the room, the two Cornelia

Eames paintings are set up and covered with some kind of cloth.

"So, the Remingtons lost the paintings in a bet?" Laurie asks my mom.

"Yes," Mom says. "Of course they weren't as valuable then as they are now, but the artist was already something of a personality. She was a...free spirit, and her lovers were some of the most prominent men of the time." She pauses. "Anyway, I was told the family of the man who won the paintings offered to give them back to the collection."

I wonder how valuable the paintings are. "Why would they return them?"

She looks at me, her eyes doing the journey from my face to my dress once again. She's already told me that I've lost weight and that she's worried about me. She sighs. "Well, the Remington Foundation depends on the income from this place. Cornelia Eames is a famous painter, so adding her work to the roster brings more people here. It helps to keep the foundation running and to postpone the inevitable day when the bulldozers come for this place."

"So dramatic." Dad laughs, looking indulgently at her, and she smiles up at him, her face lighting up. *Get a room already*, I think almost resentfully, taking a sip from the glass of champagne I took from a passing waiter. Looking around, I notice that the room isn't packed full, but the turnout is impressive. The guests are not only arty types, though it's hard to tell from the clothes since everyone is dressed up. I recognize a few socialites with well-reported interests in art, and I imagine that there may also be some distant Remington relations in the crowd.

I'm about to turn back to my parents when I see a familiar face. It lights up in recognition and makes a beeline for us.

"Rachel!" He looks surprised and pleased to see me, and I smile at him, though I'm finding it difficult to look at the handsome, familiar features. "I didn't expect to see you here."

I feel the same way. He drops a kiss on my cheek then faces my family, his manner relaxed and confident, just like his brother.

"I'm Aidan Court," he says, holding out a hand to shake my father's.

"Trent Foster," Dad replies pleasantly, taking Aidan's proffered hand. "I'm Rachel's dad. This is my wife, Lynne, and my niece, Laurie." He cocks his head contemplatively. "Any relation to Landon Court?"

"They're brothers," I offer politely.

Aidan confirms with a nod. "We had the pleasure of meeting your brother," my dad tells him, unaware that even this small reminder of Landon's existence has taken me back to the state of emotional turmoil I can't seem to escape for long.

"Landon's somewhere outside," Aidan says. "Talking with the director. He should be here any moment."

"Landon is here?" I hate how panicked my voice sounds.

"He's donating the paintings." Aidan winks. "My grandfather was a skilled gambler, winning whatnot from unsuspecting friends."

My mother gives me a concerned glance. "I wasn't aware...of the connection," she says, more to me than anybody else.

I nod slightly, even though my mind is racing, my heart suddenly beating fast enough to make me slightly dizzy. No, I'm definitely not ready to see Landon again.

"I'm going to say hello to a few people I know," Aidan says, taking his leave. "It was nice to meet you all."

"Did you know he would be here?" Laurie asks me. I've been angry with her since yesterday for leaving me alone with Landon, and her halfhearted apologies have done nothing to mollify me.

I glare at her. "No, of course not."

"I didn't know," my mom whispers. "They emailed

me the program, but...I only read the part about me giving a speech."

"It doesn't matter," I whisper back. Maybe he'll come in, donate his damn paintings, and leave. Maybe I won't have to talk to him. I take a deep breath and close my eyes. When I open them again, I see Landon walk through the doors to the ballroom, a smallish, tuxedoed man beside him. The man is saying something to him, but Landon isn't listening. Somehow, his gaze found me the moment he entered the room, and when his eyes meet mine, it feels like we're the only two people in the room.

He looks incredible of course, painfully handsome with his hair slicked back to reveal the beautiful angles of his face. In his tailor-made black tux, he seems to stand taller than everyone else, like a god amongst ordinary men.

It's probably just my imagination, I tell myself. I want to turn away, but my body rebels, compelling me to keep drowning in his gaze. Tears tease in my eyes, fueled by the unbearable yearning inside me. It feels as if I'm imprisoned by my feelings for him. I can't shake them, can't will them away. The more I try, the more they tear me up inside. It's like I'm struggling against invisible bindings and only making them tighter.

He starts to move, and it seems like he's coming

toward me. Heat sizzles in my blood, my chest tight-ening in a mixture of excitement and anxiety. At that moment, someone starts to talk on the mic, the chairperson of the board of the Remington Trust. I can't hear what she's saying. I can only see Landon, can only feel the exquisite sensation of his eyes on me.

Then I hear his name, and the spell is broken. He looks away from me as people start to clap. I watch him move to the front and begin to tell the attendees how honored he feels to be able to return the paint-ings to the Remington collection and contribute to the legacy of the place. When he's done, the director of the trust calls my mother up to talk about the two paintings and the artist. I try to hear what's being said, try to listen to the words, but the only thing running through my head is Landon, and the fact that he's only a few feet away.

I watch his profile as he listens to my mother's speech. Did he know she would be here? Even if he had, there was no way he'd have known I'd be here too. Even the fates are conspiring to throw us together, it seems.

When my mother comes back, I see him turn toward us again. One of the members of the trust approaches him and they talk for a few moments, then as the man walks away, Landon starts in our direction.

I panic. Of course he's going to come say hello to my parents—he's too polite not to—and then I'll have to stand here, smile at him, and act as if I'm not totally torn up inside.

"I'll be right back," I mutter to Laurie before hurrying away, out of the ballroom. I'm running away, but I don't care. Outside, there's a Remington House staff member to direct me to the ladies room. In the lonely solace I find there, I stare at my reflection in the mirror. My eyes are wide, my skin flushed. I wish I could pour cold water from the tap on my skin to calm my blood, to stop my heart from racing wildly.

Landon only had to look at me to make me lose all sensible thought. Why is it so hard to be in control of myself whenever I see him? My mind goes back to yesterday, to those heated words he whispered in my ear, and I hug myself tightly.

I'm tempted to leave. I could go home right now, give my parents some sort of excuse as to why I had to abandon them, and find a cab to take me to the solace of my bed. There's a persistent internal instinct urging me to do just that, and I would, if I didn't know running away is as good as telling Landon how weak I am.

It takes a couple of deep breaths before I'm sure

I'm calm and collected enough to return to the ball-room. I make my way back, desperately hoping maybe Landon will have left, that I won't have to face him.

I'm only a few feet from the doors when they open and he steps out. I stop walking, my whole body freezing at the sight of him.

He doesn't see me at first because he's facing the direction of the exits, but then, as if he senses me, he stops walking and turns to face me.

I can't look at him without feeling crushed by pain, but I can't look away either. His gaze envelops my body, reaching deep inside me to the places where all I want is to be whatever he needs me to be. I try to give him a polite, casual smile, but my heart is aching, and my face refuses to obey.

I'll never stop wanting him, I realize now. I'll never stop wanting to be with him.

It's only a moment—him looking at me, his mask dropping so that the longing in his face is plain for me to see—then the mask is on again. He turns away without a word and heads for the exit.

There is a pain in watching him go, an unbearable agony that builds in my heart and spreads through my blood until I feel like I'm drowning in it. I watch him as he walks away and I know I'm being a fool. I don't want to let him go, I *can't* let him go.

He's already at the doors. I take a step forward, toward his retreating back. Common sense screams at me to turn away, but everything else is crying out for him. He pushes the doors open and I watch them slam shut after him, like the pounding of a gavel proclaiming the end for us. It galvanizes me into action and I run forward, pushing outside just in time to see the black limo slide to a stop in front of him.

He opens the door himself and starts to get in.

"Landon, wait." My voice sounds desperate, even to me, but it works. He stops, his hand still on the handle, and turns around to face me. I'm still standing at the building entrance, and I take a few steps toward him, unsure of what I'll say when I get to him. I only know that I can't bear for him to leave.

I stop at the edge of the sidewalk, only a few feet from him. "Landon..." I make an attempt to find suitable words, but he makes them unnecessary. In two strides, he has closed the distance between us. One moment I'm searching for words, and the next his lips are devouring mine. One hand snakes around my waist while the other flexes at my nape, angling me toward him with a possessive determination that leaves me weak.

I clutch his jacket, a low moan escaping me as his tongue plunges into my mouth, moving against mine and taking control of my senses. I'm desperate to remove every last barrier between us. I'm eager to surrender every last part of me. I'm tired of fighting the way I feel. I can no sooner stop wanting him than I can stop the sun from rising, and it's no use fighting it.

Landon releases my lips, his chest heaving. I can feel the tension in his muscles, the consuming heat of his body, and his arousal, hard against my belly. "Fuck," he swears harshly. There's an edge of desperation in his voice that mirrors what I'm feeling. His hand tightens around my waist. "What are you trying to do to me?" he says roughly. "What do you want from me?"

I gaze up at his face, the face I love, the familiar features that are so endearingly perfect. His eyes are digging into mine, smoky and hot with desire. "I want you." The admission comes out in a low but determined whisper.

His chest expands. "Stop playing games with me," he warns. "Go back inside and join your family." I shake my head and he lets out a hot breath. "Or you can come with me, Rachel, and just so you know, I'm not going to stop until I've fucked you senseless."

I sway in his arms, the force of heat and arousal that surges through me at his words making me unsteady on my feet. As his arms tighten around me,

I know that, in this moment, I would go anywhere with him.

I meet his eyes. "Let's go."

His gaze darkens, his eyes flicking over my face, then he releases me and takes a step back, holding the door of the car open for me.

I climb into the luxurious interior and shift to the far side, my eyes on Landon as he slides in to join me. I can barely keep my hands to myself. I'm excited, shaking, hungry for him, unable to wait any longer to give in to what I've denied my body for far too long.

"The Swanson Court?" The limo driver's voice is an unwelcome intrusion into my thoughts. Landon tears his eyes from mine and turns toward the driver. "Just drive," he orders then presses a button to raise the privacy partition. When we're alone, he turns to me, and his eyes travel from my face, and down the length of my body. Moving so quickly that I barely have time to register his intention, he reaches for me, his hand sliding under my nape to pull my face toward his.

"God, I want you," he growls.

I sigh, feeling my nipples tightening beneath my clothes. I want him so much. I run my tongue over my bottom lip, and he groans. The next moment his tongue is sliding into my mouth, hot, demanding, hungry... I let him in with an eager moan, reveling in the taste, the feel of him.

His free hand slides under my dress, pulling up the material while stroking my thighs. His touch ignites my skin, even as my senses drown in the taste, feel, and scent of him. His fingers reach the juncture of my thighs and he presses his palm against my core, touching me through the lace of my panties. I moan against his lips, already wet, pulsing, hot, and aching for him. I spread my legs as much as my dress will allow, my fingers tangling in his hair.

He pushes the crotch of my panties to the side and slides his fingers over my wet folds. I rub my body eagerly against his fingers, going crazy from his touch. He pulls his lips from mine and holds my gaze, watching my face as he slides his thumb inside me.

I cry out, my body clenching sweetly around his probing digit, trying to pull him deeper.

"You want me," he whispers fiercely.

"Yes," I whimper, grinding my hips.

He pulls out the thumb and replaces it with two hooked fingers, stroking my sensitive walls while he teases my clit with his wet thumb. He strokes it lightly, sending sparks of sensation to my brain with each touch. "Say it," he insists.

"I want you," I cry softly. "I want you so much."

His chest expands with a huge breath and he

continues to fuck me with his fingers, pumping them fast while his thumb massages my clit. My moans are loud and uninhibited as I offer myself to him, my hips bucking wildly. When he stops, I feel like I'm going to die.

He lifts me with both hands, positioning me so I'm straddling him. I undo his pants, eager to touch him, to hold his cock in my hands, to have him deep inside me. His hands are also eager as he lifts my dress up to my waist before pulling down my panties. He gets them to mid-thigh before he loses patience and I hear them rip, but I don't care. I pull down his briefs, and he lifts his hips to help me. His cock springs free, hard and hot, thickly veined and fully erect.

"Oh, Landon." I sigh, my whole body melting with desire.

I position myself over him, throwing my head back when the wide head of his cock touches the slick entrance to my body. His hand tightens at my waist, holding me still and preventing me from sliding down his full length. I look questioningly at him, not sure why he's waiting.

"Are you ready?" His voice, like his body, is strained and tense, like he's holding on to the last remnants of his control.

"Yes." If he waits any longer, I'll have to beg. "Yes,

Landon, please."

Still holding my waist, he flexes his hips and pushes upward, stretching me sweetly as he slides deep inside.

I let out a soft moan, unable to control myself. "Landon," I cry out, my voice weak. "Oh God, Landon." I don't know how I've managed without this, without him for so long.

His hands flex, stroking feverishly from my waist to my hips and thighs. "Rachel." He closes his eyes, his chest heaving.

I brace my hands on the seat behind him and slowly rock my hips upward until just the tip of his cock is inside me. Then, shuddering with pleasure, I push back down till he's buried to the hilt again.

He lets out a harsh growl then his hands are back at my waist, gripping tightly as he starts to pump upward, the thrusts fast, deep, and hard. My whole body turns to liquid as I collapse against him, crying out as each delicious thrust fills me with delirious pleasure.

He finds my lips and kisses me deeply, stroking my tongue in time with his movements. The pleasure builds to an explosive peak and the world disappears, everything disappears apart from Landon and the wonderful sensation of his cock stroking in and out of me.

My body tightens, my insides gripping him then pulsing uncontrollably as I explode. I hear my voice crying out helplessly, saying his name as the sensations paralyze me. Landon groans, then he's moving, still inside me. He lays me on my back and continues to thrust into me, his movements almost feral, his face clouded with a raw arousal that makes me want him even more.

Heat builds between my legs again, stoked by his quickened thrusts and his voice saying my name over and over. This time, my scream is incoherent. My whole body shatters and my hips buck wildly, my heated core tightening sweetly around his pulsing cock. He rears into me with a harsh groan and I feel the warmth of his orgasm spurting inside me.

He's still breathing deeply when he pulls out of me. His arms snake around me and he nudges me upright, smoothing my dress over my thighs before adjusting his pants. My body feels light, languid, and sensual. I want to hold on to the way I'm feeling for as long as I can.

I'm surprised when he leans toward me and kisses me on the lips. This time the kiss is slow and gentle. "You okay?" he asks, pulling back to look at me. There's a small smile on his face.

My face heats a little. I feel better than okay, actually. I feel heavenly. I return his smile, watching as he pushes my wrecked panties into his pants pocket. "Yes, I'm fine."

He reaches for my hair, smoothing it with his fingers and pushing the tousled strands back from my face. His touch is so gentle that I close my eyes and lean into it. I've missed his gentleness—have missed him, period.

When he's satisfied, he lowers the partition and in a few clipped words, instructs the driver to take us to the Swanson Court Hotel.

"My parents will be wondering where I am," I muse, wondering how much time has passed since we left the Remington House.

"You're in no condition to go back there," Landon says. He doesn't look at all regretful about that fact. "Call them. Tell them you decided to leave."

"Hmmm." I frown. "What about Aidan?"

"I was already leaving when you saw me." He chuckles. "Aidan has plans to indulge in the free champagne. He told me he doesn't mind walking home." He shrugs then spends a few seconds just looking at my face. "I'm not letting you go tonight," he tells me.

My eyes flutter closed, my body shivering in anticipation. I don't argue. I don't want to leave him either. I've been punishing myself all week, and I've been walking around with a numbing emptiness that

I don't feel anymore. For the first time in days, I feel alive. This is what I want, to be with him, and there's no point trying to fight it.

His hand closes over mine. I feel the possessiveness there, and in his eyes, I see relief. *What happens now?* I wonder. Have I given my assent with my actions to his offer of a relationship? And what does that mean for me? That I've accepted to stick my head in the sand and take whatever he offers until the day I dread finally arrives?

As the limo enters the underground parking lot of the Swanson Court Hotel, Landon squeezes my hand gently. At that moment, I decide to stop thinking, to stop waiting for the end, to stop trying to protect myself from heartache and instead allow myself to enjoy the moment.

CHAPTER 7

*L*ANDON'S Swanson Court apartment is the same as I remember from that first night— still incredibly spacious, and still beautiful. It has only been a few weeks, but it feels like a lifetime. I can't resist the smile as I remember choking on my drink when I realized he thought I was a hooker. With everything that's happened since then, it seems so long ago.

On the walls, the few paintings and pictures are hanging where I remember, the photo of the ballerina still center stage. It's Landon's mother, who died in a car crash when he was nine. I study the ethereally beautiful face for a moment then turn to watch as Landon tosses his jacket on a chair. "Drink?" he asks.

I shake my head. "I'm great." I've already sent a text to tell my mom I wasn't feeling well and decided to go home. I sent another one to Laurie, telling her the truth.

Landon nods then comes toward me and takes both my hands in his. "I'm glad you're here," he says, his voice somber.

I melt inside. "Me too."

"Come on then," he says, leading me toward the stairs. I follow him upstairs, past the bedroom where we spent that first night to a larger, cozier one. There are personal touches in this room—a picture frame of his family in happier times, his tablet, some books. This is where he lives.

Landon takes my purse from me and sets it on the nightstand, then he faces me, his eyes seeming to drink me in. "I've imagined you here so many times, it's hard to believe that you actually are." His words send a flush of pleasure through me, and I tremble as he strokes my cheek. "I've missed you."

I lean my head on his chest, feeling as if a huge weight has been lifted from me. "I've missed you too," I whisper, finally free of the torture of having to pretend, of having to force myself to accept a life without him.

"I can't stop looking at you." He chuckles self-mockingly, making me smile with happiness and an aching gratitude to be so close to him again. "You have no idea how it's been for me with you across town, so close, and yet...so unwilling to have anything to do with me."

I shake my head. "I wasn't unwilling." I look up and meet his eyes. "I just...I didn't want things to get irreversibly complicated."

He laughs. "It's too late for that."

Closing my eyes, I breathe in the scent of his skin. He's right, of course. It's too late. We're already irreversibly complicated. I warp my arms around his waist, feeling his firm muscles under my fingers, and I start to think that maybe I should tell him now how I really feel, how afraid I've been that one day he'll hurt me...but I stay silent. I want to enjoy this moment for as long as possible, to ignore my fears for as long as I can.

"You sure you don't want anything?"

"Maybe some water?"

He nods. "Bathroom's over there." He points me toward a door then leaves me on my own. On the other side of the door, there's a spacious suite with a dressing room separated into two wings, and a luxurious bathroom.

I take a warm shower then towel myself dry

before going over to the dressing room. One of the wings is filled with Landon's clothes arranged in numerous racks, shelves, and drawers. It's easy to find his t-shirts, and I pick one and pull it on. It's too big for me, of course, but it's comfortable and smells of fresh laundry, and of Landon.

Back in the bedroom, Landon is on the phone. He has unbuttoned his shirt and loosened his cuffs, and there's something potently sexy about seeing him half-dressed. It's such a far cry from the impeccably clad man everyone else usually sees. I linger at the door just to gape at him for a few precious moments.

He catches me looking and reaches for the jug he's brought with him on a tray. He pours water into a glass and comes over to hand it to me.

"Goodnight," I hear him say to whoever's on the phone before he turns his blue gaze to me. "That was Aidan," he explains. "He managed to get home without falling down drunk somewhere."

He's smiling, almost indulgently, and I sigh inwardly. How could I not love him? So young and yet, so caring. He had to be a father to his little brother when he was a child himself—and still is sometimes—without any kind of resentment or self-ishness, because that's the kind of man he is.

"Aidan's lucky to have you," I tell him, meaning every word.

His lips curve. "And I'm lucky to have you here." He takes the empty glass from me and sets it down. "Nice t-shirt by the way. Looks very sexy on you." He trails his fingers down my arm, making me tremble. "Can you guess what will look better?"

I frown. "What?"

"The owner," he says with a serious face.

I burst into laughter and he joins me. There's something so intimate in that moment. If I weren't so sure about his aversion to commitment, I would almost be convinced that he felt something more than just the overpowering physical need that defines our relationship.

"I'm going to take a shower," he says, shrugging out of his shirt. "Don't fall asleep."

"I won't," I assure him, watching him walk away shirtless, the muscles of his back firm and rippling. I sigh then go over to the nightstand to retrieve my phone from my purse. There's a text from Laurie in my notifications.

There was no fooling your mom, sorry. She guessed you left with Landon.

PS Are you sure you know what you're doing?
XXXX

I debate whether to reply. I'm not sure of anything except that right now, I need to be with Landon. I wonder what my mother thinks, what she would think if I told her everything. I can't imagine her ever being as conflicted over a man as I've been over Landon. Men have always been easy for her—she still has my dad wrapped around her little finger after more than a quarter-century together.

I have no idea what I'm doing, I type in reply to Laurie's message. One day, if this ends badly, she'll probably have to nurse me through it. The thought makes me sad, and I place the phone on the bedside table and get under the covers just as Landon returns. He's wearing only dark blue silk pajama bottoms, his hair damp and tousled, the muscles of his chest making me want to reacquaint my fingers with every firm contour.

"Your workouts must be intense," I quip appreciatively, unable to tear my eyes away.

Landon sees the direction of my gaze and shrugs. "I lift a few weights and do some martial arts training when I have the time."

"Yeah, me too," I tease, rolling my eyes. "Totally when I have the time." He laughs and I continue. "Brett tried to get me and Laurie interested in working out when he started the gym," I say, giggling. "I'm just destined to be fat and unhealthy."

"How are they?" Landon's expression turns to concern.

I sigh. "It's very complicated right now."

"Emotions always get complicated." He frowns, a faraway look creeping into his eyes. "Some people make it work, but sometimes it just ends badly."

I wonder if he's thinking of his parents. His mother's love turned to jealousy then ended with her death. She left the man she loved wounded and unable to carry on even with being a father to his sons.

Or maybe he is trying to tell me that love is not in the cards for us.

Maybe because he can read the uncertainty in my face, he joins me under the covers, pulling me toward him so that my head is resting on his chest. I close my eyes, resolutely forgetting about everything else and luxuriating in his warmth and closeness, the feel of his skin against mine, and the sound of his heart beating beneath my ear. I want it to always be like this.

But it won't, that hateful inner voice makes sure to remind me.

I push the thought out of my mind. I'm going to be satisfied with taking as much happiness as I can get from being with him, for now.

I feel his hand stroke my hair. "You know I'll give you anything you want?" he whispers in my ear. "You know that, right?"

Why does that statement make me happy and sad

at the same time? "You don't have everything," I reply.

His chest moves. "Don't walk away again," he murmurs. "Don't."

I'm silent, and his hand stills in my hair. I feel his heartbeat quicken as he waits for me to respond. "I won't," I say softly. "I won't."

I FALL ASLEEP IN LANDON'S ARMS, PEACEFULLY, without any miserable dreams where I'm alone and yearning for him. He's everywhere, his arms cradling me, his scent in my nose, his warmth all around me.

When I wake up in the morning, he's already up. I open my eyes to see him standing at the door to the dressing room, already dressed in one of his tailored shirts and pants. He's fixing his cufflinks and watching me as I stretch.

"Good morning," I say with a grin.

He smiles. "I was trying to decide if I had the heart to wake you up. You looked like you were having a good time."

"I was." I slept like a baby. I stretch again then remember that I have to get to work. I grab my phone off the nightstand to look at the time. "Christ! I'm going to be late! I have to get home to change."

Landon's smile is calm, almost teasing. "Don't worry." He walks toward the bed. "Joe already got your clothes. Laurie was very helpful."

I calm down. "Really? What are you, some sort of super boyfriend?"

His gaze turns serious. "I'd settle for boyfriend."

My heart warms as a small thrill moves through me. Landon's looking at me, waiting for me to say something. "You never told me what it is you want that I can't give."

I shake my head. "It's not..." I stop, not sure what to say. I know I don't want just any relationship; I want the possibility of love at least, and an assurance that I won't just be another woman passing through his life. I take a deep breath and watch as he comes to sit on the edge of the bed.

"I know I have a lot of baggage," he says, "and all the other issues you know about."

He's talking about his dreams, the result of being right there and helpless the day his mother died. My eyes mist. "I don't care about any of that," I tell him. I don't care that sometimes he wakes up at night crying out, still struggling to save his mother. I don't care that by his own admission, years of therapy didn't do anything to make him less wounded. I care about the man I know he is.

"Every other woman wanted something from

me...commitment, some sort of relationship...but I've offered you that, Rachel. I didn't even have to try, because it's what I want, more than anything, to know that I can be sure you're mine."

His. I search his face. "And you, will you be mine?"

Landon chuckles, and his hand travels up my arm. The movement is a light caress, and yet unmistakably sexual. My body reacts, instantly filling with desire. "I'm already yours," he admits, his voice low.

What does that mean? That sexually he is bound to me, that he needs me physically the way I need him?

"It's just sex, Landon. We're still practically strangers."

"So we'll get to know each other." He sounds confident, but I'm not. I can see us together for a few weeks, maybe months. We'll get photographed and attend events together, and then one day, I'll watch him do the same things with some other woman.

The thought fills my heart with a severe, wrenching pain. I rise to my knees, leaning toward him, threading my fingers through his hair. If I'm going to be with him, I have to take advantage of the one way I know to control the pain and the uncertainty. I press my lips to his, running my hands over his chest through the cotton of his shirt.

A soft groan escapes him, and he moves one hand to the small of my back while the other strokes my thigh. My body fills with heat and I let my lips drift to his ear. "I need you," I whisper.

A deep breath shudders through him then his lips are on my neck, my chest, his hands stroking me everywhere. He pulls the t-shirt over my head, leaving me naked. His eyes caress my body almost reverently, his gaze like a heated touch, making my skin burn and my breath come short. Desire pulses between my legs. When he's like this, when we're like this, I don't have to think about what the future holds.

"Rachel." He says my name like it's a prayer. He moves, rising to his knees in front of me. His hands cup my breasts then squeeze gently. I moan and reach for the front of his pants, the outline of his rigid erection visible through the material. I undo his fly and pull down his briefs, eager to feel the evidence of my effect on him. I curve my fist around him and stroke him gently, loving the feel of warm, silky skin stretched over his hard length.

His eyes close and I lower my head, adjusting my body so I can take him in my mouth. As my lips close over the sensitive head of his cock, he lets out a low groan. He only allows me to suck on him for a few moments before he pulls out of my mouth and lifts me bodily, pushing me back on the bed. He doesn't bother with the rest of his clothes. Still on his knees, he pulls me toward him by my legs, until the head of his cock is positioned at the entrance to my body.

I press my hips forward, and he slips inside me. He groans again, and my eyes flutter to his face. The brazen arousal in his expression sends an urgent pulse between my legs. "Please, Landon," I urge. "Fuck me now."

I don't need to say it twice. He pushes inside, filling me up, chasing away every other thought but how good he feels, how big he is, and the sweet sensations when he starts to move, his thrusts slow and exquisite.

He releases his hold on my legs, letting them fall on the bed. I brace my feet and grind my hips, meeting him thrust for thrust. His hands stroke my thighs, my belly, my hips, his fingers caressing my heated skin. Finally, he moves one hand between my legs, finding my clit and rubbing it in sweet, maddening circles.

The room is full of the sound of my moans. With each deep stroke of his cock, I feel myself going a little crazy, pleasure building inside me like a dam ready to burst. I hear myself moaning, saying his name, begging.

"You like it." His voice is an aphrodisiac to all my senses. "You like it when I fuck you like this."

"Yes," I moan, my body tightening in ecstasy. "Yes."

"Come for me, baby," he growls. "Let it go."

My climax bursts out of me like an explosion of pleasure and relief. I scream his name, my hands gripping the sheets like my life depends on it. He keeps thrusting through it all, his movements getting harder and faster as my body pulses around him. He grips my thighs and groans, coming so hard I feel his whole body vibrate.

Afterward, he drops my legs and leans over me, his chest heaving.

"God!" he breathes then pulls out of me and lies back on the bed beside me. "Oh God."

I turn to him, unable to hide my satisfied grin.

He gives me a look, one beautiful eyebrow going up. "You should wipe that smile off your face if you have any plans of getting to work today," he warns. "I could do this all day."

"Who's stopping you?" I tease.

He laughs. "You're insatiable." Getting up from the bed, he turns toward the bathroom. "I'm going to repair the damage you've caused," he says, gesturing to his clothes. "And I think I'll definitely need a big breakfast after this."

I watch him disappear, still smiling. Then I take a moment to luxuriate in the pleasure flowing through me. *I can do this*, I think happily, getting up to join him in the bathroom. *I can live with this.*

CHAPTER 8

*W*HILE I'm in the shower, Landon cleans up and changes into a fresh suit. I hear him leave the bathroom before I finish, and I wrap myself in one of his robes and pad over to the dressing room to find the clothes Laurie sent for me. The ivory sheath dress—one of my favorites—is hanging from the rack. My shoes are on the floor beneath it, and my change of underwear is inside a small shopping bag, placed on one of the shelves beside my handbag.

I dress quickly and run Landon's comb through my hair before securing it in a quick braid. In the bedroom, I toss my phone and the purse from last night into my bag then make my way downstairs.

Landon is in the kitchen, seated at the island.

There's a pot of coffee with eggs and light fluffy pancakes. The delicious smell reminds me that I haven't eaten since early last night. Landon's eyes flick over me when I join him, showing the quick flare of desire that always does things to my insides.

"You didn't snap your fingers and conjure breakfast out of thin air," I remark playfully. "Even you don't have those powers."

"I don't, but I have a dedicated chef in the hotel kitchen." He pulls out a seat. "Eat. You're almost late."

"I know." I take the proffered seat and pour myself some coffee, adding a generous serving of cream and sugar. The pancakes are delicious, and the eggs are heavenly enough to make me sad when my plate is finally empty.

"What are you doing this weekend?" Landon asks.

I give him a naughty smile. "You, if I'm lucky."

"If I'm lucky," he corrects, chuckling. "I have to work this weekend," he tells me. "I'm going to Newport to look at a property."

Disappointment floods through me. "So you'll be gone the entire weekend?"

He nods.

I frown, realizing that I've been looking forward to spending the weekend with him. I hadn't considered what a busy man he was; that's something else I have to keep in mind, I tell myself, now that we are officially in a relationship. I have to make sure I don't become that girl, waiting for him to have time for me.

"I want you to come with me," he says.

"Oh." I'm delighted, but also wary. "But you'll be working."

He gives me a meaningful look. "Not all the time."

I raise my brows. "And when you are, what will I be doing with myself?"

He strokes a finger over the side of my mouth, flicking a spot of sauce from my lips. "You'll be waiting, naked, in bed." He sounds like he's teasing, but he looks serious. I consider the image. It's tempting for sure, but deep down, I suspect that the surest way to hasten the end of our relationship is to become his idle arm-candy.

I shake my head. "I don't think so."

"How can I convince you?" He leans back. "Just me and you, alone, on the beach, the sound of the sea, the gorgeous sunsets..."

I shrug casually, as if the image he's painting isn't filling me with slack-jawed anticipation. "What's in it for me?"

"Rest and relaxation? And some poor shmuck who can't look at you without getting a hard-on?"

I giggle. "Fine. I'll come."

Landon grins. "Good. Now we'd better go before I give in to my baser instincts and do what's on my mind."

"What's that?" I ask, getting up.

His lips lift in a small smile. "Something that'll result in neither of us leaving for work anytime soon."

Ah.

∼

"DON'T FORGET LINGERIE," LAURIE ADVISES.

"What?" I look up from the overnight bag on my bed to where she's sitting at my desk, holding a Pringles tube.

"Lingerie. Something sexy." She shakes her head at my cluelessness.

I look at the deep blue bikini I've already packed; there's also shorts and a t-shirt, a summer dress, and my favorite LBD. Landon didn't ask me to pack anything specific, but I'm covering all my bases.

"Okay." I go over to my dresser and retrieve a set of sheer lingerie. I imagine Landon's face when he sees me in it, and the thought makes me smile.

"You're glowing," Laurie observes. Since that last text message where she asked if I was sure of what I was doing, she hasn't questioned my decision to be with Landon. In fact, she seems happy about it.

I look up and meet her eyes. I feel like I'm glowing. The excitement, the happiness I feel even though nothing has really changed...it's almost embarrassing.

"I know, right." I sigh. "It's pathetic."

Laurie frowns. "No, it's not. Rach, you're happy. That's what matters. Sometimes you just have to enjoy stuff while it lasts instead of overthinking and ending things before they begin."

I nod. "You're right."

"Aren't I always?"

"No!" I narrow my eyes threateningly. "I still haven't forgiven you for leaving me alone with Landon the other day. Seriously, that was a betrayal of trust."

She's unapologetic. "If it has anything to do with how happy you are right now, then I'm not sorry."

I give up. "Have you spoken with Brett yet?"

She is silent.

"You know you can't give him the silent treatment forever."

"What if he was right and we do need some time apart?" She sighs. "I'm tired of always being mad about the same thing, Rach. He's not going to change, and neither am I."

"Laurie..." I sit on the bed facing her. "You're not seriously thinking about...walking away, are you?"

"I don't know." She frowns and looks down at her hands. "Forget about me, I'm just confused."

"What will you do while I'm gone?" I ask. "Will you go home?" She'd mentioned going to visit her parents upstate.

"I'm just going to study," she says. "Thankfully I won't have my annoying cousin around to distract me."

I stick out my tongue. "We both know who the annoying one is."

We both laugh. "It's going to be fine," I tell her softly, after the moment of mirth has passed. "No matter what happens, we're going to be fine."

She nods, and just then my phone starts to ring. It's Landon.

"You set?"

"Yeah, almost."

"Joe is on his way over to pick you up," he tells me. "I have a conference call, but I'll be done in about twenty minutes, so he'll swing by the office to get me."

"Okay."

"Fine." He seems reluctant to get off the phone. "So, I'll see you soon."

"Yeah."

"Okay."

"You should get to your conference call," I tell him, smiling.

"I know." There's a deep chuckle from his end, but he makes no move to end the connection.

I laugh. "Seriously, I'll see you soon."

"Hmmm, yeah. Soon."

Laurie rolls her eyes and leaves my room, laughing softly as she closes the door behind her.

"Okay, I'm going to go now," I say determinedly. "I have packing to finish."

"Okay." There's a long pause. "What are you packing?"

"Sheer lingerie," I tease.

"Now I most definitely have no desire to get off the phone." He pauses. "Are you going to describe it to me? Give me something to think about for the next few minutes."

"No. *No.*" I laugh. "I'm getting off the phone now."

"Okay, okay." He's laughing too. "I'll see you."

After our conversation, I can't wipe the silly grin off my face. I love him. It isn't possible that there'll ever come a day when I won't be in love with him. *You're setting yourself up for an excruciating heartbreak*, a warning voice whispers in my head. The thought is saddening, depressing, but not enough to take away the excitement, the reckless elation of knowing I'll soon be with him.

A few minutes later, there's a knock on the door. It's Landon's driver, Joe, who also doubles as some sort of bodyguard. He's probably very skilled, I think now, or else Landon wouldn't trust him with his safety.

Suddenly fretting about imaginary scenarios where Landon would need protection, I wave goodbye to Laurie, who's already nose-deep in one of her unattractive law books. I follow Joe downstairs to where the gleaming black car is waiting on the curb.

Joe doesn't say much, and the drive is quiet all the way to the entrance of the Swanson Court Tower, Landon's downtown high-rise building, which houses the offices of the Swanson Court International. The memory of my first time here rises unbidden into my mind, and I bite back a smile. I'd been so mad at him, and yet, after our encounter in his office, I stopped struggling against the fact that I was helplessly attracted to him.

I'm still smiling when Landon emerges from the building, looking as immaculate as he did in the morning. He says something to the doorman then strides purposefully toward the car, joining me in the back and bringing with him that slight hint of his cologne coupled with his aura of inescapable sexual magnetism.

"Hello sexy," I say with an appreciative smile.

"You're the sexy one," he says with a grin, leaning over to place a kiss on my lips. "What were you smiling about?"

I shrug. "Nothing, just memories."

"We have some of those," he muses.

"Yes we do," I agree. We've only known each other for such a short time, and yet he has taken over almost every part of my being.

It's a long drive, and somewhere between talking about plays we've seen, arguing about which movies were better than their book adaptations and which ones were not, and me confessing that I've never been able to see constellations, I fall asleep with my head on his lap.

∾

"WE'RE HERE."

The whisper is soft against my ear, and Landon's warm breath stirs the hairs on my neck. My eyes flutter open. It's dark outside, and we're parked in the drive of a beautiful house. Landon has his arm around my shoulders, his hand gently caressing my arm.

I stretch slowly. "How long have we been on the road?"

"Four hours," he replies, "and you've been asleep about two of those." He waits while I smooth my hair. "You ready?"

I nod and he gently removes his arm from around me then opens the door on his side just as Joe comes to open my door.

Immediately I'm hit with the smell of salt and surf. I can hear the distant sound of waves, though I can't see the sea from where we are. The driveway is paved and edged with shrubs up to the steps that lead to the porch. There, a wide, green door leads inside, while the porch stretches across the whole front of the house.

"Do you own this too?" I turn to Landon, remembering the beautiful house in San Francisco.

"No." He takes my hand. "It belongs to a friend. He loaned it to me for the weekend."

"You have friends?" I tease, laughing. I've only ever met one of his buddies, the irrepressible restaurateur Cameron McDaniel. "And here I thought you were a robot."

He looks hurt. "You met Cameron."

"I knew you'd play that card," I reply. "One friend. That's pathetic."

"This makes two."

I shrug, eager to maintain my high ground. "Still not healthy." I follow him to the front door. "How's Cameron, by the way? And Julia?"

"They're still heavily pregnant." Landon opens the door and lets me go in before him. Inside, the décor is simple and almost rustic with comfortable furniture, polished wood floors, a modern kitchen, and sliding glass doors from the dining area to a wooden deck overlooking the ocean.

"Your friend is lucky," I tell Landon. "I'd live here and pretend to be writing a book, just so nobody would ask why I never leave home."

Landon laughs. "You'd miss your job."

I shrug nonchalantly. "I wouldn't have to deal with arrogant billionaires nudging my boss into sending me on assignments just so they can seduce me."

A smile plays on his lips. "One day you'll forgive me for that."

I give him a coquettish look. "What makes you think I'm talking about you?"

He makes a sound like a growl. "If anybody else tried to pull a stunt like that with you, I'd probably..." He shakes his head. "I don't even want to think about it."

His possessiveness amuses me, and also stirs a small flame of pleasure inside.

I hold out my hand to him. "Let's go to bed," I say softly. "I'm tired."

~

WE MAKE LOVE, SLOWLY AND SWEETLY, HOLDING on tightly until sated and exhausted, we both fall asleep. In the morning, I'm awoken by the cries of seagulls. Landon isn't with me in bed, but I find him on the back patio, watching the waves as they crash against the sand. He's wearing only a pair of pajama bottoms, the well-defined muscles of his back disappearing at the waistband, and the outline of his firm butt very clear through the light material.

I burrow into his back, plastering my body against him. "Aren't you cold?"

"Not anymore." He relaxes into me. "Good morning."

"Hey," I reply. "How did you sleep?"

He turns around so he's facing me. "Perfectly."

It wasn't his nightmares that woke him then. I sigh, satisfied, and lift up my face to place a kiss on his lips.

He kisses me back, his hand stroking my waist through my robe. "You must be hungry," he says when he releases my lips. "Let's eat."

I follow him to the kitchen where he whips up an

omelet and pancakes with the expertise of a professional chef, a skill he picked up while spending most of his growing-up years in a hotel.

"Yum," I tease. "I'm going to get used to you making me breakfast."

"Why not?" he says with a grin. "You have my skills at your disposal, babe." He gives me a meaningful look. "All my skills."

His tone tells me what skills he's talking about, and I bite my bottom lip, shifting in my seat, suddenly wanting nothing more than to go back to bed with him.

"I have to get to work now," he says regretfully, as if he can guess what I'm thinking. "I have a phone call with my lawyer and some documents to appraise before I go look at the property."

"Oh..." The morning stretches out in front of me. "All right."

"There's a caretaker you can call if you need anything." He shows me the card with the number by the kitchen phone.

What could I possibly need? The house seems to be stocked with the necessities, at least. After eating, we clean up after ourselves. Landon remains on the patio with his laptop and phone, sliding effortlessly into his work mode. I take my laptop to the front porch, settle on one of the cushioned wooden chairs, and start to do some of my work for the coming week. It's mostly reviews, filler pieces, and some editing work, which describes most of what I do at Gilt Traveler.

After about two hours, I look up to see Landon standing at the door, watching me.

"Hey." I stretch languidly.

"Hey." His eyes flick to the laptop on my lap. "How's it going?"

I shrug. "So so."

"I'm about to leave," he informs me. "Why don't you come with me so you can tell me what you think?"

"Me?" I laugh. "I'm not a real estate analyzer."

"You don't have to be," he says seriously. "I'd like to know what you think."

I shrug. "Okay, if you insist." I get up from my chair. "What is it, anyway?"

"An old ocean-front hotel. It has historical value and, I suppose, sentimental value to the owners. They proposed a partnership."

I frown. "But you own your properties outright, don't you?"

He nods. "Usually, yes."

"So, are you going to partner with them?"

"That's what I'm going to decide today." He takes my laptop from me. "If I'm going to pour money into the place, I want to be sure it has a chance, and that it's going to be run like any other Swanson Court establishment."

As in, with unstinting care, maintenance, and top-class service, like all his hotels.

"When are we leaving?"

He eyes the robe I'm wearing. "I was going to take a shower, and I wondered if you would join me."

"Well, if you insist," I say with a smile, letting him lead me back into the house. Inside the well-equipped bathroom, we undress each other and enter the shower stall. Landon sets the temperature with a frown of concentration on his face that would be comical if he weren't so sexy. Then, he starts to soap my body, from my neck to my back, then my breasts, where he spends an inordinate amount of time—not that I have any intention of complaining. He soaps me until my nipples peak and tighten, and then he moves down to my thighs.

When I'm thoroughly lathered, I take over from him, pouring a generous amount of soap into my palms. I rub it over his chest, running my fingers over his taut muscles and firm skin then going to his back before reaching for his hard buttocks. When I reach for his cock, he's already hard, and I curl my fingers around him, sliding my hand up and down his length, the soap providing a slippery lubrication. He makes a sound somewhere between a groan and a sigh and leans back under the spray, letting me pleasure him. The spray of water gets rid of the soap, but I continue stroking him, getting down on my knees to take his cock in my mouth.

He buries his fingers in my hair, his fingers gripping the wet strands and directing the movement of my head. I suck him as deep as I can, feeling him at the back of my throat before I slide back to flick my tongue over his sensitive tip.

I feel his thigh muscles bunch, his belly hardening and tensing. I suck him deep again and his hips start to flex, the movements in time with my head, stroking his cock with my tongue. I look up and meet his eyes just as I cup his balls gently.

He groans. "You're going to make me come."

In response, I suck harder. He makes a sound like surrender, his eyes closing as he pumps into my mouth, over and over, until his muscles tense and he comes with a loud groan.

"Fuck." He sighs, his chest heaving as I rise back to my feet. He moves me gently so my back is against the tiles then he gets on his knees, hooking one of my legs over his shoulder. He devours me hungrily, his tongue and lips hot and wet against my pulsing clit. He nuzzles my inner lips then licks me slowly. The next moment, his tongue is stroking the pulsing entrance to my body, pushing inside, tasting me before going back to flick teasingly over my clit.

I'm screaming his name, wild, my back rubbing against the tiles, my legs so unsteady I have no idea where or how I'm getting my balance. His tongue flutters over my clit again, teasing me until I'm close to the edge, then he closes his lips around the mass of nerves and sucks lightly on it. The pleasure is so intense that I almost pass out from the incredible climax that rocks my body.

I'm still reeling from my orgasm when he gets to his feet. His cock is hard again, shockingly erect and lined with pulsing veins. I don't offer any protest when he lifts both my feet from the floor, wrapping my legs around his waist. He plunges into me, his cock hitting every single nerve inside me.

My hands flutter over his chest as he starts to fuck me. His face is set, his muscles bunched tight under his skin. My back rubs against the tiles as he thrusts hard again and again, and the steam from the shower mixes with the sweat misting on my skin. Pleasure envelops me, making my blood surge. I cry out his name as another orgasm rocks through me, the powerful surge of his cock and the sweet warmth of his climax taking me over the edge.

It seems like a long while before we both recover, holding each other under the spray as warm water cascades over us. I feel languid and sensual, totally satisfied. Back in the bedroom, we dress each other. Landon zips up my yellow patterned dress and gets on his knees to slide my feet into my heels. I help him button the long-sleeved shirt and tuck it into his gray pants.

He combs his hair then sits on the bed to watch me blow-dry mine and brush it to obedience.

"You're beautiful," he says.

My heart actually flutters. "Thank you."

He gets up and takes my hand, his fingers caressing mine. "We'd better go."

Outside, the smell of the sea is invigorating. Joe and Landon's car from last night are gone back to New York, but there's a car in the garage, a shiny, two-door, Italian sports car.

Landon looks at it and grins widely.

"What?" I ask.

"Alex—the guy who owns this place—he thinks the world of this car." His grin widens. "He's probably having a heart attack at the thought of anybody else driving it."

Cars are not really my forte, but even I can see that it's a splendid machine. "Then why did he agree to let you?"

Landon arches a brow at me. "Because I can be persuasive."

I chuckle. "Don't I know it?"

Inside the car, he hands me a small leather case with the bold insignia of a popular fashion designer embossed on the top. Inside is a pair of stylish shades. I put them on, and he does the same with his own pair. They're aviators, and they make him look like a rich playboy, and I tell him so.

He raises one eyebrow. "I was born awesome, baby," he says with exaggerated swagger, making me giggle.

Our destination is a three-story hotel along the beach, the Regency Grace, according to the mounted sign, and even from the exterior, I can see that it's an old building. Landon drives to the entrance and exits the car, and I watch as he surrenders the keys to the uniformed valet, once again utterly captive to how beautiful he is, how graceful, how hot.

Landon catches my stare and smiles, something carnal in his face promising me all sorts of pleasures for later.

He starts to tell me what he knows about the hotel. Originally built at the turn of the century to take advantage of the popularity of the location as a vacation spot, the architects designed it to evoke the character of the gilded-age mansions dotting the area. There have been two additions and renovations, Landon tells me, with a real effort made both times to maintain the character of the building.

I can see what he means. It's not hard to imagine the place as part of Newport in the gilded age. Graceful white columns are topped with carved moldings, the cream walls are saved from monotony by white edged windows, and balconies dot the upper floors. The landscaping at the entrance is neat and colorful, but despite everything, there is a sense of something that's beautiful but long past its prime.

At the main entrance doors, there's an older couple waiting to meet Landon. He introduces them to me as the McLarens. Mrs. McLaren is the current owner, and she manages the place with her husband. They're both in their seventies at least.

"Call me Lucy," she urges when Landon introduces us. She's a sweet old lady with her silver hair in a low bun, her eyes still sparkling with liveliness. "What a lovely thing you are!" she gushes at me before turning to her husband. "Isn't she Dave?"

Dave McLaren's face is lined, but still handsome. He gives me a charming smile as he shakes my hand. "Without a doubt," he says, agreeing with his wife.

Landon raises his brows in my direction; there's an amused smile on his lips, but I ignore him and thank the old couple for their compliments.

In the lobby, everything is clean and polished. It's

clear that day-to-day maintenance is not the problem, but rather the undeniable aura of age that even the efforts of the management have been unable to mask.

There're a few guests milling about, and a few couples with children. "Dave will show you around," Lucy tells me. "There's a lot to see. I'm going to steal your beau for a few hours so we can talk in my office." She smiles. "You don't mind, do you?"

"No, of course not," I reply with a smile. I turn to Dave. "I'm looking forward to seeing the place."

There's a lot to see. The hotel has potential— even my untrained eyes can see that—but it's also clear that it's suffering. The spa is closed indefinitely for maintenance, as is the expansive putting green. The private bungalows that line the oceanfront are also empty. There's a restaurant on the deck overlooking the ocean and the white sand beach; only there do I see an impressive number of customers which, Dave tells me, is because the seafood is popular with the locals.

Afterward, we all have lunch on the deck. The McLarens recommend a fresh seafood dish that's really excellent, and we talk about Newport, the old private mansions now open to the public, and the tourists that troop in every summer. There is no more talk of business, even though it's clear that the

McLarens are hopeful that Landon will make a decision that favors them.

Finally, Landon thanks them for their time and they walk with us to the entrance, waving goodbye as the valet brings the car around.

On the drive back, Landon puts on some evocative instrumental music, and I close my eyes, drowsy from lunch. "What did you think?" he asks.

I pause to gather all my impressions about the place. "It has a lot of potential," I tell him, "but it feels so old...like they've tried their best, but they don't really know how to bring it up to date."

Landon nods. "You're right. That's the impression I got too."

"So." I frown, thinking of the hopeful old couple. "What will you do? Will you invest in it?"

He pauses. "Not if they want to keep running the place. It's admirable that they've held on for so long because everything else out there is owned by corporations. That's why I decided to see for myself, even though my team had already put up a red flag."

"Oh." I don't blame his team, but I can't shake the image of the McLarens in my head. Maybe I'm too emotional for this business of making money.

Landon continues. "If I'm going to put the Swanson Court name on the hotel and inject my money into it, they're going to need new management, new ideas, and thorough refurbishment to make it less ancient and more..." He searches for a word.

"Classic," I offer.

He looks at me and smiles slowly. "Exactly."

I listen as he talks about what he thinks the place needs. He's incisive, calculating, thorough, and I'm glad I'm seeing this side of him. Hotels are in his blood, I realize, but they're also in his heart.

"You're so sexy when you talk shop," I say after a while.

He glances at me, a grin on his face. "Who knew? I'll have to do more of that when I'm with you." There's a pause. "Thanks for coming today."

"I didn't mind."

He nods. "But I'm glad you were there, and that I can talk about my work with you."

It makes me happy too, to be able to share that part of his life. "I'm glad you're glad," I tease.

He laughs. "I'm going to make you dinner," he offers. "What would you like?"

I smile at him. "I'd eat anything you made."

"Okay." He thinks for a moment. "How do you feel about grocery shopping?"

The thought of him pushing a cart through the aisles of some grocery store is so incongruous with the *image* of Landon Court that I almost burst out laughing. However, he's serious, and he soon pulls into the parking lot of a chain supermarket.

"Isn't there someone who can do this for you?" I tease, "so you don't, like, injure yourself or something?"

"You obviously think I'm an invalid," he says. "You're wrong. Just watch me."

Inside the store, I watch him as he carefully selects from the offering of fresh produce, meat, and vegetables. When he lifts two bunches of celery and turns to me with a *What do you think?* expression, I can't resist taking a picture with my phone. I show it to him, almost doubled over with amusement.

"Nobody would believe that was you."

He shrugs and tosses one bunch into the cart. "Not forceful, ruthless, and single-minded enough," he says.

I recognize the words from some of the articles I've read about him, and I link my hand with his. "Well, at least I know what a sweetie you really are."

That makes him smile, and we walk together to the counter. I'm enjoying the fact that besides his insane good looks and the commanding aura he effortlessly exudes, we could be any regular couple, out shopping on a Saturday night. There's something infinitely pleasurable in the fantasy.

Back at the house, I help him make dinner,

mostly ogling him because he's incredibly sexy even when he's doing something as basic as cooking.

We eat outside on the back patio, and afterward, we lie under a blanket on the large porch swing while Landon tries in vain to help me recognize the patterns in the night sky. When I keep laughing and insisting that I see nothing but random stars, he gives up and entertains me with stories from his college days instead. I fall asleep lying on his chest, his voice in my ear, and it's the best feeling in the world.

CHAPTER 9

LANDON'S moans wake me up. We're in the bedroom, he must have carried me there after I fell asleep. My eyes adjust to the dim light from the windows, but I can't move, and I soon realize why. Landon's arms are tight around me, his breathing fast, and his muscles as tense as if he's getting ready to run or fight.

"Let me go," he mutters. The words are low and garbled, immediately followed by what sounds like crying.

I try to move, but his arms only tighten as he struggles in his nightmare.

"Landon," I whisper, as close to his ear as I can get. "Landon, wake up. You're dreaming."

My voice seems to reach him. His body stills and

163

his face gradually relaxes as his breath slows to a normal rate. I watch him go back to a peaceful sleep, wondering what I can do. I remember what he told me weeks ago—he saw therapists throughout his teenage years, and if that didn't help, what could?

Landon's eyes flutter open and he stretches his hand to switch on the bedside lamp. He sees that I'm awake, and a frown crosses his brow. "What's wrong?"

"Nothing," I reply, not sure that there's any point in telling him that he'd been dreaming again.

He studies my face for a long moment. "I woke you up with the nightmares, didn't I?"

I sigh. "Yes."

He takes a deep breath and throws his legs over the side of the bed, sitting with his back to me. He leans forward, burying his face in his hands, and then he pushes his fingers through his hair. I reach for him, wanting to place a comforting hand on his back, but he's already getting up from the bed.

I drop my hand back on my lap. "Where're you going?"

"I have some reports to read." He doesn't look at me. "Go back to sleep."

I can't go back to sleep, and I don't want to, not when I'm worried about him. "You don't have to go, Landon. We can talk about it if you want."

He shakes his head. "I don't think so."

I frown. "Don't you? Or maybe you still think it's none of my business?"

He faces me, and the lost, haunted expression on his face makes me ache for him. "Landon," I urge gently, "talk to me."

He comes back to sit on the bed and takes my hand. "You already know what the dreams are about. The accident. I watched my mother burn in that car, and I couldn't do anything. Everything changed when she died. My whole family fell apart, my father became a shell, and my brother wouldn't say a word. In my dreams, I want to save her. I want to save her so badly, and it feels like it would be possible if only I could get away from the person holding me back."

I squeeze his hand. I've seen the pictures from the old newspaper reports. He carried his little brother out of the wreckage, but his mother had been unconscious, and when the car started burning, some concerned observer prevented him from going back for her.

"Tell me about her," I say quietly. "Your mother."

He doesn't reply immediately, and his silence makes me wonder if he'd rather not talk about her. Then he sighs. "She was the most beautiful woman in the world, at least to the nine-year-old boy I was. She used to practice at home sometimes, and watching her dance was like watching an angel." He pauses.

"She had the softest, gentlest voice, and she liked to laugh."

He looks at me and smiles. "She loved Aidan, and she would play with him for hours, no matter what kind of silly game he wanted. She loved to read too. My earliest memory is of her reading to me. I guess she also had a temper, especially when she fought with my dad, but he always knew what to say to her, how to remind her that she was the most important person in the world to him."

I listen to his voice, fighting back tears. "They sound like lovely people."

"They were," he replies. "Then the accident happened."

I touch his back. "Landon, there's no shame in the fact that it haunts you. Most people would never forget if something like that happened to them. You survived. You saved your brother. You were strong for him. It's something to be proud of."

He doesn't reply. *He's still leaving*, I think sadly. Why did I think talking to me would be enough to heal him even of the slightest of his wounds?

"I wanted to go back." His voice is low, almost too quiet for me to hear. Unlike the last time he spoke to me about the accident, his pain is visible, almost palpable. "I didn't want to leave." He lowers his face into his hands again then lifts it back up with a sigh.

"I prayed so hard for anything to happen, anything to make us go back, at least until my father came back. I knew that once he arrived he'd make it up to her somehow. I didn't know what I was asking for, just any reason for us to go back home and wait for my dad. Then something happened. We crashed."

I get up on my knees and put my arms around him from behind. "Landon," I whisper soothingly. "You were a child."

"Don't you think I know that?" He laughs bitterly. "But it didn't stop me from torturing myself for years."

I place a kiss on the cool skin of his shoulder then get off the bed, sliding to my knees in front of him. "Look at me," I whisper. "I'm glad you told me, but it wasn't your fault. You didn't wish the accident to happen. You were just a child afraid of his parents separating. I'm sure you made a thousand more wishes that didn't come true. It wasn't your wish that caused the crash. It was an accident."

He nods, silent.

"Whenever you start thinking like that nine-year-old boy again, just remember how much you loved your mom, how no wish you made could have caused her any harm."

A ghost of a smile crosses his lips. "Yes ma'am."

"I'm not joking," I tell him.

"Neither am I." He pulls me up onto his lap. "You're incredible," he says. "An angel."

I nod, accepting the compliment in place of the endearment I know I'll never hear from him. "You need to get back in bed. Get some sleep."

He lays me down on the bed and stretches out on top of me. "I know what I need," he murmurs, rocking his hips against me so I can feel the unmistakable evidence of his arousal, "and it's not sleep."

"You're insatiable," I whisper, melting into him.

"You're irresistible," he replies.

I cup his face in my hands. *I love you*, I say silently, the words burning a fever in my mind, and I press my lips against his, pouring all the desperation of my feelings into the kiss. His response is to wrap his arms around me and roll onto his back so I'm on top of him, still kissing him, my legs straddling his hips.

"You're like a drug, Rachel," he says when I stop for breath. "You make me forget everything, everything apart from you."

I don't reply. I'm also addicted to him. Trying to survive without him was like cutting out a part of myself, and the withdrawal symptoms almost drove me crazy. "When I'm with you, I feel like nothing is missing." I sigh softly. "Like everything finally fell into place."

It's the closest I can get without actually telling

him I'm hopelessly in love with him. He pulls me toward him and claims my lips again, his erection pressing against the inside of my thigh. I pull away just long enough to gently guide him inside, sliding down until his full length is sheathed in me.

His eyes cloud and his lips form my name.

I close my eyes, almost unable to bear how good it feels. *It won't last*, I think sadly, painfully aware that being like this will never mean the same thing to him as it does to me. The sobering thoughts make me determined to get as much pleasure as I can from him. I guide our movements, riding him hard, using the physical sensations to push all thought from my mind. Soon the pleasure is too intense for me to think at all. Landon rears up, gripping my hips, his lips greedily sucking on a nipple as I ride him faster and faster. We come at the same time, holding tightly to each other. There are tears in my eyes from the exquisite pleasure, and also from the inescapable despair.

WHEN I WAKE UP IN THE MORNING, LANDON IS still asleep, and I spend a few moments greedily drinking in his features before I go to the kitchen to try to rustle up a passable breakfast.

Cooking is not one of my strengths, so after checking the cupboards and analyzing the stuff remaining from yesterday, I make a big production out of French toast and chopped fruits before Landon joins me.

He's freshly showered, and somehow, devastatingly sexy in a purple terrycloth robe. He has his tablet under his arm and is talking on the phone. He grins at me and pours himself coffee, still talking to whoever's on the other end. He pauses long enough to place a kiss on the back of my neck before he makes a plate for himself and goes out to the patio to continue his call.

I watch his retreating back with an unhappy frown then settle down to eat breakfast alone. I finish up, stack the dishes, then go to the patio to peek. He's sitting on one of the deckchairs, still talking on the phone. Now he has his tablet on his lap, going through whatever it is that he's discussing. He looks up and sees the frown on my face then smiles apologetically and blows me a kiss.

I make a pouty face and go back inside. He told me before we left that he would be working, so I can't complain. After I shower, I consider calling Laurie to gossip, but I decide I can do that after I get back. Thinking about her reminds me of the lingerie set I never got to wear, so I find it in my bag and slip into the sheer lace and satin ensemble.

It's definitely sexy, and looking at my reflection in the bathroom mirror makes me want to go out to the patio and make Landon forget what he's working on. I'm sorely tempted, but I decide to let him work, instead concentrating on finding something to read on my e-reader. After flicking through the many titles, I settle on a fantasy novel, and soon I'm immersed in a world of prophecies, dragons, and magical powers I wouldn't mind having. When Landon comes into the bedroom a few hours later, I'm thoroughly engrossed.

He sits at the edge of the bed. "What're you reading?"

I look up from the screen long enough to give him a side eyed glance. His eyes are glued to my scantily clad body. *Serves him right*, I decide. "Are you done working?"

He pulls his eyes to my face. "Yes."

"Well, now I'm busy," I tell him, going back to my book.

"I can see that." I hear the smile in his voice as he takes one of my feet in his hands, massaging it gently. "Are you mad at me?"

"Why would I be?" I turn a playful scowl in his direction. "You told me you were going to be working. Now, if you don't mind, someone has a guild of evil magicians to challenge and defeat."

Landon laughs. "Sounds critical. I wouldn't dare to interfere with something of that magnitude, with potentially far-reaching consequences."

He continues to massage my toes, and it feels so good, I have to bite back a sigh of pleasure. "What're you doing?" I ask suspiciously.

"Nothing," he says innocently. "Go on, defeat those evil magicians." He pauses, and then continues with a teasing note in his voice. "Though I don't think you're suitably dressed for something so important."

"Really?" I laugh.

"Yes," he replies, still massaging my foot. "For one, you wouldn't have just this thin lace covering your breasts. Your nipples are visible, tempting...an explicit invitation to suck on them."

As he speaks, my nipples tighten, poking through the lace. I press my thighs together, a wave of arousal settling between my legs.

"And your thighs," he continues, his hands drifting from the magic they're working on my toes to trail their way up to my calves, and then to my thighs.

"What about them?" I whisper.

"They're barely covered, just a little lace. Who can look at them without thinking about sex?" He pushes my legs apart and palms me through the lacy crotch of my lingerie. I'm already soaking wet, and now he knows.

"You're not reading anymore," he points out smugly.

I breathe and turn my face to the screen of my device, my eyes unseeing. I steal a glance at him and he meets my gaze, his face straight as he hooks a finger into the crotch of my panties and shifts them to the side.

I'm already panting softly, my lips parted in antici-pation. I'm totally exposed to him, and I can almost feel the heat from his lips just a few inches from my sex.

"You can't stop reading now," he teases. "Think of those evil magicians."

The only evil magician is him. I bite my lip, my stomach fluttering as desire pools between my legs, but I manage to give him a challenging glare and turn my eyes back to my device. Now I definitely can't see a single word on the screen, and I'm not trying to. My whole body is waiting, and when Landon's lips touch me, it takes everything for my hands to keep holding the device.

He licks me leisurely and I know he's enjoying himself. His tongue strokes my inner lips, making me tremble, then he rims my cleft, licking and stroking before pushing inside me. I bite down my moan, holding it back until his tongue travels back up to my clit, fluttering over the sensitive nerves. I cry out and toss the e-reader, leaving my fingers free to twist in Landon's hair.

He goes on and on, untiring, until my body is weak and shuddering, almost passed out from pleasure. He uses his fingers as well as his tongue, pushing them inside me, teasing all my sensitive spots, until I'm just a mass of nerves crying out in unbearable pleasure.

I come over and over until I'm begging him to stop. When he finally raises his head, he's grinning, and I can hardly move. My legs are wobbling, my whole body throbbing, my voice hoarse from screaming in exquisite pleasure.

"Let's go for a walk," he suggests, as if he didn't just give me multiple orgasms. "We can't leave without at least exploring the beach

HE'S RIGHT ABOUT THE BEACH—IT'S BEAUTIFUL. The sand is white, clean, and eager to deliver a treasure of different types of shells. The sound of the ocean is soothing, and the cry of seagulls lends an interesting oddity to the atmosphere. We walk barefoot at the edge of the surf, reveling in our solitude, taking selfies with the sunset in the background, and enjoying the feel of sand against our soles.

"It's so beautiful," I tell Landon, watching the waves traveling up to the shore.

"You're beautiful," he tells me.

I sigh. He somehow expects women not to fall in love with him and demand commitment when he says stuff like that to them?

"What's on your mind?" he asks, correctly gauging the shift in my mood.

"Just building up my arsenal for resisting your charms," I say with a shrug.

He looks hurt. "My charms are irresistible."

Laughing despite myself, I push his chest lightly. "You're not very humble."

"No." He grins. "I have you beside me. I have every right to strut like a peacock."

I roll my eyes, and he pulls me toward him and places a soft kiss on my forehead.

We walk back to the house to eat the lunch that's delivered by the caretaker, then we make love on the porch swing. It rocks with our movements, its gentle swing lulling me to sleep after.

When I wake up, the sun is setting over the horizon, casting a vibrant deep orange glow over the water and the sky. It's breathtaking, and Landon allows me to admire it for a while before letting me know it's time to leave.

A hired driver is already on his way to take us to the airport, where Landon's plane is waiting. So, we get ready, silently gathering our things. It's almost as if we're both feeling the same thing, an unspoken reluctance to go back to the city, back to our lives, leaving the idyll of our weekend behind.

CHAPTER 10

*W*HERE *are you?* the text arrives just as I get into the car waiting for Landon when we arrive in New York. It's from Dylan, my baby brother, and it's accompanied by an angry emoji.

What's up? I type in reply, pleased and surprised. Dylan isn't the best communicator in the world. He buries himself in his video games and his studies and mostly resists our attempts to dig him out.

I'm at your place with Laurie, he texts back. *When are you coming back?*

Already on my way, I reply. *Will be there in minutes. Wait for me!!*

"My brother's in town," I tell Landon, smiling excitedly. He met Dylan once, and they actually hit it

177

off, which wasn't usually par for the course with Dylan.

Landon nods, and I lean closer to him, tempted to burrow as close as I possibly can and prolong the memory of our wonderful weekend. "Do you see him often?" he asks.

I shrug. "Not as often as I'd like, but we usually pick up where we left off."

He laughs then pulls me in so my head is on his shoulder. "I don't want to let you go," he murmurs in my ear.

I know what he means. Through the short flight and even now, I've been thinking the same thing, how much I wish the weekend didn't have to end. My body softens, melting into his. "I had a great time too."

When we're almost at my place, he strokes my arm. "Will you change your mind about coming to San Francisco for the opening of the new hotel?"

I smile shamefacedly, recalling how I reacted to his earlier invitation. "Of course I'll come."

He nods. "I'll leave town sometime this week, but I want to see you every day before I leave."

"Every day?" I echo, so pleased I'm almost ashamed of myself.

"Is that too much?"

Never! I grin. "I'll consider it."

He's laughing. "Let's have dinner tomorrow," he says. "When you're not working, I want you to be with me."

"Yes boss."

He chuckles but doesn't say anything. At my apartment, he carries my tiny weekend luggage upstairs, kissing me goodbye at the door.

I watch him walk down the stairs, taking them two at a time, and then he blows me a kiss before disappearing from sight.

I take a deep breath then turn to unlock the door and let myself into the apartment. I'm so happy I feel like I'm floating. I have to tell myself not to hope, not to want any more than I've already settled for, but it's hard to listen.

Inside, Dylan is stretched out on the couch, and Laurie is seated on the floor, laughing at something he said.

"Look who's back!" she exclaims, not getting up. She wiggles her eyebrows meaningfully. "How was your weekend?"

Dylan unwraps his lanky body from the couch. He looks like my dad, but with the same green eyes as me and my mom. "Laurie says you went on a romantic getaway with your boyfriend." He looks serious. "I feel bound to challenge him to a duel to defend our family honor."

Laurie is giggling. "Pistols or swords?"

"Both?" Dylan abandons his straight-faced expression and doubles over with laughter. He takes a few steps to where I'm standing and we hug, then he pulls me toward the couch. "We're drinking wine and sharing secrets," he tells me. "You have to join, and in case you're wondering, I'm not going to fight your boyfriend." He does a dignified-old-man face and pats my head. "You're of age."

Laurie breaks into giggles again and Dylan joins her.

I shove him gently. "How much wine have you guys had?" I exclaim, joining Laurie on the floor while Dylan throws himself back on the couch. Laurie hands me an empty glass and pours me some of the red wine they've been drinking. "What are you doing in the city anyway?" I ask Dylan.

"I came to see a show," he replies.

"Huh!" I crane my head to look at him. "What show?"

He tells me the name of some rock band I've never heard of.

"Did he go with a girl?" I ask Laurie.

She nods slowly.

I turn to Dylan. "Tell me more. I'm your sister."

He holds back for a while, and I tease him mercilessly until he volunteers a few details. Her name is

Kelly. She's also premed. They came to see a show. She went home after, and he decided to stop by my place. It's not much, but from Dylan, it's a whole lot of information.

He allows me to keep teasing him while we order takeout and then we stay up late watching episodes of *The Avatar*. Dylan spends the night on the couch and is still asleep when I leave in the morning.

He's going straight back to school, a detail that would break my mom's heart if she finds out that he came all the way without going home.

My walk to the office is invigorating. The air is crisp and smells of all the different flavors of New York, and I allow myself to dwell on how different I feel from just a few days ago, how the knowledge that I'll see Landon in the evening makes me want to break into song as I walk.

A few blocks from my office, my phone rings. Pleasure rises inside when I see that it's Landon.

"Good morning," he says.

"Good morning."

"Did you have a good night?"

I smile. "Mmmhmm."

"Dream of me?"

"What do you think?"

He sighs. "Your brother still around?"

"Yeah. He's leaving today."

Landon is quiet for a moment. A horn blares loudly close to me. "Where are you?" he asks.

"On my way to work. I'm a few blocks from the office."

"You're walking?"

"Yeah," I reply, surprised at his tone. "It's the only way to keep my weight from catching up to my IQ."

He doesn't laugh at the joke. "You and Laurie walk together?"

I see where he's going. "Sometimes, other times she leaves earlier than me."

"I'm not convinced it's safe," he states, confirming my idea.

"Well, it is. I've been doing this for two years."

He is silent, and I hear him expel a breath. I understand how safety is an issue for him, but I'm not a billionaire hotelier. I don't need a bodyguard.

"When are you leaving the office?" he asks.

I tell him.

"Joe will pick you up," he states, an edge of finality in his voice. "Just let me know when you're about to leave.

"Landon, it's not necessary."

"I think it is." His tone is firm, not the tone of the lover from yesterday, but of the man who's used to being obeyed. "Your safety is important to me," he continues, his voice softening. "The more people know who you are to me, the more unreasonable it becomes for you to traipse around with no security at all."

I keep quiet, feeling defiant. "It's not like we're taking out an announcement or anything like that."

There is a short laugh from his side. "We won't need one."

He sounds so certain that I start wondering how many times he's been through this, the excitement from the gossip columns whenever there's a new woman in his life.

"Just let Joe pick you up," he says. "I'm having enough nightmares about how porous your apartment building is as it is."

I bite my lip. I love my apartment, and the building, and the fact that I live in a cute old walkup. "Fine."

"I'll send you his number so you can call whenever you need him." When I don't answer, he continues, "I'm probably going to work a little later than I planned tonight." There is a regretful note in his voice. "But I'll call you."

"Sure," I reply, disappointed. "See you whenever."

He sighs. "Where are you now?"

"Almost there," I tell him.

"Good," he says. "I'll see you soon."

AT THE GILT BUILDING, INSTEAD OF HEADING toward the elevator bank, I walk across the lobby, past the waiting areas, toward the gallery. Here, pictures from Gilt's history line the walls. There are black and white daguerreotype kind of images from the turn of the century when Francois Gilte, a French publisher with unproven stories of being descended from aristocrats, arrived in New York to launch a fashion and style magazine, the first incarnation of Gilt Style. After a few years of immense success, he went bankrupt and lost the magazine to a corporation, but he was retained as the editor-in-chief, and Gilt continued to grow, adding more publications to its stables.

I move from picture to picture, the iconic editors over the years, women who ruled New York fashion with one look, word, or preference for an accessory, women I grew up reading about in Aunt Jacie's issues of Gilt style. There are pictures of models, actors, society women, even renowned authors being honored for their stories in the Gilt Review long before they were famous.

There is something about being at Gilt, I think as I study the pictures. It's like being a part of history, of creating art that touches millions. Even if I never end up at the Review, I doubt that working at some other literary magazine would ever feel as good as being in the Gilt family.

"Rachel."

I turn around and see Chelsea eyeing me with concern. "I saw you on my way to the elevators. She eyes the pictures. "Hobnobbing with the ancestors?"

I wrinkle my nose. "Yeah."

She smiles. "It's awesome, isn't it? Well, the history, not the actual being here—but it's better than someone trying to talk me into a season of *Rich Kids of Kentucky*." She shudders.

"You'd look awesome on TV, though."

She makes a gagging sound. "Never." She peers at one of the pictures. "One of these women once described my mother as a heifer in diamonds," she says with an uncaring shrug then turns to look at me. "I saw a picture of you on some gossip site, kissing Landon Court outside the Remington House." She peers at me. "You guys made up?"

I nod.

"Good." She narrows her eyes. "But I still want to go clubbing, whether you're miserable or not. When are we going?"

I sigh, ashamed of having forgotten. Chelsea's refusal to toe the line of idle heiress meant she didn't have many friends among people like her. She found most society people boring after a while, but that didn't stop her from being lonely. "I'm sorry," I say remorsefully, making an apologetic face. "I forgot, but we should go sometime this week. I'll tell Laurie."

Chelsea nods, satisfied. I am too, glad of the opportunity to make plans that don't include Landon. For someone who couldn't be counted on for the kind of long-term commitment I craved, I was in danger of making him the center of my life. I needed to go out with the girls, hang out and have fun without the shadow of my feelings hanging over my mind.

Chelsea starts to tell me about her flirtation with her hot neighbor; she still suspects him of being some sort of security specialist hired by her dad to protect her from would-be kidnappers. We're still talking when we get to our floor and exit the elevator. It's early, so there's almost nobody around, and we're walking in the direction of our offices when a door opens and Jack Weyland walks into the corridor.

I'm surprised to see him. It's only been a few days, but the time spent with Landon has pushed him out of my mind very completely. I remember our last meeting with a feeling that's almost like embarrassment, and his expression goes from surprise to something like pain before he gives us a small nod and walks in the opposite direction.

"What was that about?" Chelsea asks, her eyebrows going up.

"I have no idea," I reply, feeling conflicted. Once again, there's that feeling of loss, because every single feeling I ever had for him and every dream I built around us ultimately ended in nothing. Even after everything he put me through, I can't help but feel concern that I hurt him, but sadly, there's absolutely nothing I can do about it.

LANDON CALLS IN THE AFTERNOON TO CONFIRM that he'll be working late, so when I'm done for the day, I do as he instructed and call Joe to pick me up and take me home. Laurie isn't in yet, so I microwave my dinner and watch some TV in solitude before going to soak in the tub.

My mom's call doesn't surprise me. I knew that one way or another she'd find out about Dylan's visit. She chides me for not telling her he was around.

"You know I'd have loved to see him," she frets.

"You saw him last weekend, Mom, and we were just hanging out."

She sighs. Dylan is the one guy whose relationship with my mom is different from all the others. He's the one who has had her wrapped around his little finger from the moment he was born. "I get it," she says. "At least I'm trying to. So, are you back together with Landon?"

The switch from Dylan to Landon takes me by surprise. "I... Yes. For now."

"So it's not serious?"

"I...I don't know. Sometimes it feels like it could be."

She sighs. "In other words, it's what you want, but you're not sure if he wants the same thing."

I don't reply.

She is silent for a long moment, probably wondering how she failed to pass the man-eater gene to me. "When you told me you guys were no longer together..." She sighs. "Sweetie, you shouldn't let yourself get too emotionally involved with someone if it's not the same for him."

Too late. "What if I'm already too involved?"

I hear her sigh. "It should never be about the man, sweetheart. It should be about how he makes you feel. If you're not sure how he feels about you, how happy can you be?"

How happy can you be?

I leave the bath after our conversation. For a while, I try to read, but give up when I can't concentrate. When I'm with Landon, I am happy. Sometimes the cloud of uncertainty interrupts the happiness, but it's nothing compared to the hollowness and pain I felt those few days when we weren't together.

I can't bear the thought of being without him again, or the knowledge that when the day finally comes for us to end, it won't be my choice. It will be because he doesn't want me anymore, or because I've asked for some kind of commitment he can't bring himself to make.

I fall asleep with all that on my mind, and I don't even hear when Laurie comes in.

I wake up in the middle of the night to Landon sliding into the bed with me. Before I can ask any questions, he pulls my body to his, plastering me against his warmth. He smells clean and fresh like he's just had a shower, but his skin is warm and naked against mine.

"Hi," I whisper, all my fears vanishing now that he's here with me.

"Hi," he replies before he lowers his head to kiss me.

His lips are sweet and warm against mine. I kiss him back, pressing my arms around his back to pull him closer. "I missed you today," he says when he frees my lips.

"When you weren't bossing me around."

He rolls on top of me, covering my body with his.

"You're the only boss in the room," he whispers, trailing his lips from my chin to my neck. He pulls up the top I'm wearing, and I lift my arms to help him pull it over my head. Then he lowers his head to my breast, his lips closing over one nipple. He sucks on it while cupping the other breast, rubbing the nipple with the pad of his thumb.

Sensation takes over my body, and I'm instantly aroused. The familiar ache starts low in my belly and travels between my legs, and I move my hips, grinding my body against his. I part my legs, needing more than anything for him to touch me, and as if he can read my mind, he obliges. One hand slides between us to cup my sex, stroking me through my underwear and making me moan in pleasure.

"Did you think about this while you were at work?"

"Every minute," I say with a sigh, rubbing myself against his fingers. He pulls my panties out of the way and touches my sex, stroking and rubbing with just the right amount of pressure.

My hips rise, and he pushes his fingers inside me, then he spreads them, seeking and finding the nerve endings guaranteed to send me over the edge. He rubs my insides leisurely, sighing when my walls contract around his fingers.

I reach for his cock, my fingers closing around the

stiff length. He is rock hard, like velvet over warm steel. "You're so hard," I whisper.

"Because I've been waiting all day for this."

"Me too," I tell him with a sigh. "But I can't wait anymore. I want you inside me."

He groans at the words, and his fingers slip out of my sex. He pulls off my panties then lifts me up, pulling me up by my arms so we're facing each other, on our knees. He hugs my upper body to his, lifting me while with his free hand, he positions his cock between my legs before letting my body slowly slide down till he's completely sheathed inside me.

He holds me there for a few seconds, unmoving, my breasts pressed against his chest, my body filled with him. I squirm, my inner walls clenching around him, but he holds me still, whispering soft endearments in my ear, kissing my throat, my face, my lips.

I let out a desperate moan, my hips straining, trying to ride his cock, but he tightens his hold on me. One hand slides over my buttocks and cups my butt, kneading the soft flesh for a few delicious moments before his fingers slide between my cheeks. One finger rims the tight opening there, stimulating and teasing at the entrance before slowly sliding inside.

My whole body contracts with pleasure. I grind my hips desperately, groaning my need. Landon continues to tease me with his finger, rimming me from behind while his cock throbs, unmoving inside me.

"You're so sweet," he whispers. "I love being buried so deep in your hot pussy."

I cry out helplessly, my body clenching, eager for him to fuck me, even as his teasing at my rear opening intensifies. "Please," I beg frantically, desire driving me insane. "Please Landon, fuck me now, fuck me hard...oh God!"

His hips move, flexing hard, and I can feel the warm softness of his balls pressed against my wet center. Then he pulls out and drives in again, this time even deeper, his finger still stimulating me from behind.

All my senses are on overdrive. Everything is centered on the sweetness of his cock inside me, the decadent pleasure from behind, and my clit rubbing against him every time he thrusts hot and deep into me. I'm utterly helpless. All I want, all I need is for him to go on fucking me—as long as he wants, any way he wants, everywhere he wants.

And he does, thrusting into my pulsing body over and over, pushing me closer and closer to an insane height of pleasure. I surrender my senses to him, feeling nothing but the sweet sensations of his skillful touch.

My climax tears out of me with a tortuous cry and my whole body explodes. He continues to drive into me until I come again, and again, and my whole body feels weak and spent, liquid and boneless. Only then does he let go of his control, his abandoned groan as he fills me with the heat of his climax spurring me to another final orgasm.

He falls back on the bed, me on top of him, sweaty and exhausted. I feel tender, but so suffused with pleasure that I'm practically floating. I fall asleep listening to his heartbeat as his chest rises and falls. *I love you*, I say silently inside my head. *I love you so much.*

His arm tightens around me, almost as if he heard, but when I wake up in the morning, he's already gone.

CHAPTER 11

I catch Laurie in the kitchen about to leave for work. She's already made coffee and poured some in a travel mug.

"Lookee you all glowing," she teases. "I would ask you about your night, but since I heard..."

"Shut up," I mutter, pouring myself a mug of the steaming black coffee. "You let him in?"

"Yeah, he called me when he was on his way up." She frowns. "He said he tried your phone a couple times but you didn't pick up."

"I was asleep." I only saw Landon's missed calls when I woke up to find him gone. "I wasn't expecting him to come over. He told me he was working late."

"Well, you kept him working late."

I give her a threatening glare, but she grins, unfazed.

"How would you like to hit the clubs Friday night?" I ask. "Chelsea invited us."

She shrugs. "Why not? If anybody ever needed that kind of fun, it's probably me."

"It's not that bad," I say encouragingly. "You know it isn't. Brett's probably hurting as much as you are."

She doesn't reply. She still hasn't allowed him to explain about the girl from the deli. He's probably taking it really bad that they might actually be at the end of their relationship. I'm tempted to plead with Laurie to give him another chance, but I'm not sure if it's because I miss the familiarity of both of them together or because I really think he's the best for her.

I get ready for work, and when I get downstairs, Joe is waiting in the car. I pause for a moment to admire the sleek lines of the obviously expensive vehicle. Do I really want to arrive at work every morning in a chauffeured CTS? That's a conversation I might have to bring up again with Landon.

Before Joe can come around to open the door for me, I take the few steps to the car, pull the handle, and freeze in a mixture of pleasure and surprise when I see Landon waiting inside.

Grinning like an idiot, I join him in the back. "Hi

sexy," I drawl, admiring how mouthwatering he looks in his three-piece. He's the quintessential image of the billionaire, as different from the uninhibited man who fucked me senseless last night as it's possible to be.

"Good morning," he replies, his gaze traveling over me like a caress.

"I dreamed about you last night," I whisper, teasing his blue silk tie with the tip of my finger. "It seemed very, very real."

He raises a brow. "If you thought for a moment that was a dream, then I have to work harder next time and make sure you're really awake."

Next time? I suck in a breath. "Are you going to make a habit of slipping into my bed?"

"I'm going to make a habit of going to bed with you every night." He raises a hand to stroke my face gently, and I sigh. "Let's have dinner at my place tonight," he proposes, his hand finding its way to my thigh. The light caress is enough to make me wish we were anywhere else, somewhere private.

"Okay."

"Will you spend the night?"

Will I? I hide my smile. I'd probably go back there with him right now if he keeps doing what he's doing with his hand. "Yes, of course."

"Come over straight from work," he says. "Don't bring anything."

I frown. "Why not?" I'll have to go to work from his apartment in the morning and will need a change of clothes at least.

"You'll see," he says cryptically, reaching into his jacket pocket to retrieve a keycard, which he hands to me. "We added some security measures at the hotel, but this will allow you to access my apartment whenever you want."

I take the card from him. He's just given me the keys to his apartment. I don't even know what to say. I want to ask if he's ever given any other woman so much access to him. I want to hope it means something. I smile and slip it in my purse. "Thank you."

"I'll leave for San Francisco on Thursday morning," Landon tells me, sounding regretful. "A plane will be here for you Saturday morning. I'll have someone take you to the airport."

Thursday to Saturday—two whole days when I won't see him. I swallow the ache, the twinge of sadness. "I'm looking forward to it."

"To me being gone?" He's teasing, and there's a small smile playing on his lips.

"No." I chuckle. "To joining you on Saturday."

He squeezes my hand. "Can you go out tomorrow night?"

"Yeah." I search his face. "What's happening?"

"A friend of mine." He grins when I raise my eyebrows. "A friend of mine is launching a new product for the American market, some new European champagne brand. There's a mixer, and I want you to come with me."

I realize there'll probably be press there, people who'll talk about the fact that I was there with him. I would be there as his girlfriend. If I still have any misgivings, any desire to hold back, this is my chance to make a U-turn.

"Of course." I smile at him. "I'd love to."

He smiles back. Joe slides into the front of the Gilt building and stops the car.

"Enjoy your day," I whisper, placing a quick kiss on his lips before reaching for the door handle.

"Wait." Landon's hand snakes out and catches my arm. He leans forward and kisses me properly, for long enough that I can feel the shocks of pleasure in my toes.

"I'll see you tonight," he says.

I nod and stumble out of the car on unsteady legs. I can hardly wait.

∾

AFTER WORK, JOE IS WAITING TO DRIVE ME OVER

to the Swanson Court. I send a quick message to Laurie on my way over, telling her I won't be home all night.

At the underground car park, I thank Joe politely before following the security staffer who directs me toward the elevator. The card Landon gave me ensures that when I get to the penthouse floor, the doors slide open, letting me into Landon's apartment.

I'm almost overwhelmed again by the size and beauty. Like the rest of the hotel, the architecture reflects the time when it was built, and the décor is luxurious, yet comfortable. After I go upstairs to leave my bag in Landon's bedroom, I come back to the living room to look more closely at the pictures of Landon's family. I'm charmed by a photo of Landon as a towheaded but serious-faced child, and one of the whole family laughing at the beach.

Later, I wander to the balcony, and then back inside to place a call to the hotel restaurant. I order dinner on hotplates for when Landon arrives. After that, there's nothing else to do but wait for him, so I lie on one of the sofas. To stop myself from dozing off, I start to play with my phone.

I still get emails from the search alert I set up for Landon, but I've been ignoring them for the most part. At first I didn't want any reminders of him, and then later, I was determined to avoid something that felt very much like spying on him. Now I see that another alert has popped up, and out of curiosity I decide to open it, thinking it might be the picture Chelsea was talking about.

The first news story is about the Swanson Court Hotels, and I frown as I read the first paragraph describing how Landon is opening the Gold Dust amidst rumors and accusations of coercion in the acquisition of properties.

The publication is a reputable online news source, so I know it's not just gossip. I frown, wondering how serious the accusations are, and why Landon hasn't let on that there were any problems.

The next story is older, on a gossip site, and there's a grainy picture of me and Landon at the airport from Sunday with a headline screaming about billionaire Landon Court and his 'companion.'

I'm still laughing about that when I open the next story. This one is newer and has two images with no accompanying writeup. In one of the pictures, I see Landon and some woman in front of the SCT Building. The second one has Landon and the same woman having dinner at a restaurant. In the first shot, Landon is holding a car door open for the woman, and she's smiling up at him. In the second one, their faces are close together and they're both laughing, her hand on his arm. I look for the date of the article and my heart goes cold. It's from yesterday.

I stare at the woman's face, trying to remember if I've ever seen her before in all the other articles I've read about Landon, but I can't recall the face from anywhere. The quality of the images is not so good, but from what I can see, she's beautiful, with glossy black hair hanging halfway down her back and full, red lips. I close my eyes. Last night, when he said he was working late, he was meeting with this woman.

He lied to me.

And then he came to my apartment. My memories from last night are so clear that I can still feel him slipping into bed with me, freshly showered after spending his whole evening with her.

I'm suddenly trembling. The thought of Landon leaving me at some remote date is something I've schooled my mind to expect and accept, but the idea of him being intimate with another woman while lying to me and making me feel like I matter to him...

It's not something I can bear.

I try to breathe, to stay calm, but I'm helpless against the deep clawing desperation threatening to drown me, the realization that I'm nothing more than a temporary indulgence, a plaything.

I allowed him to suck me back into his life. I buried my head in the sand and developed a false sense of security. Now every intimate moment we shared seems like a lie.

Feeling like I'm suffocating, I leave the sofa, going toward the elevator in the foyer. At first I just want to leave the apartment, to go outside where I can escape the surroundings that are so full of him.

When did dinners with beautiful women become 'working late?' What kind of egotist is he if he'd gone out of his way to pursue me, only so he could lie to me and show me that I meant nothing to him?

At the ground floor, I hurry through the front lobby. Under the awning over the sidewalk, the doorman gives me a questioning glance, as if wondering whether to call me a cab. I ignore him and start walking. It's just beginning to get dark, and the air is changing, getting colder.

I pass several buildings, blind to everything but the worst of the possibilities playing through my head, making me want to cry. I don't consciously start walking toward home until I realize that the only thing I have with me is my phone. I have no money, no keys to my apartment, even the keycard Landon gave me is back at his place, so I can't go back to get my things.

There are other people on the sidewalk, some meandering, others walking with purpose. I blend into the crowd, my face down, my eyes teary, wondering if the pleasure of being with Landon is worth the pain I'm feeling.

How much did I really mean to him if he could lie to me just so he could spend time with someone else?

I've been walking for a while when my phone rings. I switch it off without looking at the screen, not confident of my ability to have a rational conversation, especially with Landon.

I remember my mom's advice. *It should never be about the man, but about how he makes you feel.* Right now, I feel like crap. The lack of certainty, the inevitability of heartbreak, the depth of emotion I feel, emotions he'll never return...it hurts. It wounds me in ways I never thought possible.

Yet being without him wounds me more.

I don't want to be stuck in this state forever, wanting more than he can give, unable to ask for it, and yet unable to walk away.

But what can I do?

I walk for what seems like hours, although it can't have been that long. When I reach home, my legs are aching as much as my heart.

Landon is standing on the sidewalk in front of my building, his hands deep in his pockets, his eyes scanning the street. They settle on me as soon as I turn the corner, and I see his expression change from tense anxiety to profound relief.

He rushes toward me. "What happened?"

The desire to walk into his arms wars with the desire to walk away. He places soothing hands on my shoulders. "What happened?" he repeats softly.

That's when the tears start to fall.

Landon hugs me tightly then retrieves a white handkerchief from his pocket and wipes my face. "I got home and you'd left, but your things were there." He looks at me, concern etched in his features. "What's wrong?"

In the face of his tender concern, it's hard to tell him that I walked out from his apartment because I saw a picture of him with another woman. Suddenly, I feel immature and foolish.

I breathe "I..."

"Are you all right?"

"I'm fine." I step away from his arms, trying to regain my composure. "Where were you?" I ask softly. "Where were you last night?"

Landon frowns. "Where was I?"

"You told me you had meetings, but I saw a picture of you having dinner with some woman."

His whole body seems to stiffen. "You what?"

"I saw you." My voice sounds small and petty, even to me. Why hadn't I considered that he would be here, waiting for me? I breathe. "I saw you with your dinner date, and you looked like you were having a good time."

He looks hurt and confused. "And you left?" he exclaims, his voice sounding incredulous. "You didn't think you needed to ask me about it before walking away?"

I close my eyes. "You lied to me about where you were last night. Maybe I didn't want to wait to be lied to again."

He laughs, and it's a frustrated, angry sound. "I didn't lie to you. I had meetings. I had a meeting with her, just like I had meetings with other people over the course of the day. I decided to conclude our meeting over dinner to save time. Are you satisfied, or would you like a fucking list of every single person I spoke to yesterday?"

I feel as if he slapped me. "I'm not supposed to care that you were out with someone else when you told me you'd be working? I'm not supposed to care that you didn't think to mention it to me until I saw it online? Fine then." I shrug. "I don't care."

He glares at me then turns away, pulling out his phone from his pocket to make a call. "You can come back now," he says curtly before disconnecting and making another call. "She's here," I hear him say, then after a pause, "No, she's okay."

He pushes the phone back into his pocket and

glowers in my direction. "Do you realize I had my driver searching the streets for you? Do you realize your cousin was worried about you? You preferred to take a walk across the city, at this time, alone, because you saw a picture online. For fuck's sake, Rachel! Do you know what could have happened? How would I ever fucking forgive myself if anything happened to you?"

His voice is raised, his jaw hard and tight, but he has that sad, haunted look in his eyes, the one I saw last weekend, the night he told me about his mother. Shame descends on me when I realize what I've done. She left too, based on something someone told her, something she didn't wait to confirm.

I cover my face with my hands. "Landon, I didn't think..."

"No you didn't." He looks resigned. "You were too eager to indict me." He spears me with his eyes, and I see the accusation in the blue depths. "Are we still at this stage, Rachel? Are you still looking for excuses to walk away?"

I don't reply. His car appears on the street and comes to a stop beside him, Joe behind the wheel.

"You can go up now." Landon's voice is emotionless. "I'll send your things later tonight."

He turns toward the car, going to open the back door. I know what I've done, and the realization of how much I've hurt him settles like a weight on my shoulders. If he leaves now... I can't bear to think that he might never come back.

"Wait," I say, my voice breaking on the word. "Please, Landon."

He stops and turns to look at me. My eyes are wet, and I feel as if I'm hurting all over. "I'm sorry," I whisper.

He doesn't move, and I inhale, a tear rolling down my cheek. He mutters a curse, and then he's walking toward me, holding my body to his with one hand while he wipes the tear from my face.

"You're going to drive me crazy," he whispers.

"I'm sorry," I repeat, burying my face in his chest.

He breathes. "Are you sure you won't go up? Laurie was very worried."

I shake my head. "No. I want to come with you."

We don't say much during the drive back to his place. I can tell he's deep in thought, and I wish I knew what he was thinking about. I switch my phone back on and see all the texts from Laurie asking where I am, and I respond with an apology and an assurance that I'm all right.

She replies immediately.

What happened?

Long story. I'll tell you later.

Confused face

Then. *Landon was out of his mind with worry. You'll have to try harder to convince me that he doesn't feel something for you, maybe something as deep as what you feel. Just my opinion.*

I look from my screen to Landon's face; he's looking out the window, the line of his jaw illuminated by the lights from outside the car. His face is unreadable at the moment. If he feels anything now, I assume it's probably annoyance, impatience, and disappointment that I didn't care to think my actions through.

I don't reply to Laurie's last text. I don't know what to say, and I don't want to give myself any hope. I may not have gone into this clearheaded, but I know I have to be strong enough not to punish myself—or him—for the decision I made to stay with him.

In his apartment, the dinner I ordered is in the kitchen, still warm in the hot plates. Silently, Landon pours me a glass of wine then disappears upstairs. When he returns, he has changed out of his work clothes and is wearing sweats and a t-shirt.

"You should go change," he tells me. His voice is

sober, and he hardly looks at me. "I'll lay out the food."

Silently, I do as he says, making my way upstairs to his bedroom, where my bag is still sitting on one of the chairs. In the bathroom, I wash my face, then I go into the dressing room. I'm about to reach for one of his t-shirts when I notice that the other side of the large space, which was empty the last time I came over, now has clothes hanging from the racks, clothes that, from their varied colors, cannot possibly be for a man.

Don't bring anything, he'd said, and now I realize why. There're at least two weeks' worth of clothes for the office, a few casual ensembles, and evening wear. There's nightwear folded on the shelves, lingerie in the drawers, some simple jewelry, and shoes too— everything I need so I never have to hesitate before coming over.

I sit on the carpeted floor and cover my face with my hands, fighting back tears. All my suspicions and fears now seem so ridiculous. There is no doubt that he wants me in his life, no doubt that I'm important to him, but while he was opening his home and himself to me, I did the one thing I promised him I wouldn't do: I walked away.

Without waiting to hear his side.

I compose myself and start to look for something

to wear. I finally choose a sleeping shorts and tank top ensemble that closely resembles a pair I have at home over the collection of smooth satin nighties. I return downstairs, and Landon is not in the living room. Following the sound of a TV, I find him in an adjacent room that looks like a den and has a huge couch facing a widescreen TV. He has set out dinner on the coffee table, and on the TV screen, a popular period drama is showing.

He looks up when I enter the room, his eyes going over my clothes. "I hope you don't mind," he says. "I thought having a few things here..."

"I don't mind," I whisper. "They're all perfect."

"I'm glad you like them." His voice sounds distant, and it makes me ache. "The shoppers came highly recommended, but in case there's anything else you want, or something you wish to change, I'll make sure you have their contact details."

"Okay," I murmur. There's a lump in my throat, so much I want to say, but the events of the evening seem to have built a wall of awkwardness between us. I join him on the floor in front of the couch and we eat. At first we're silent, then we talk about the show, about the actors, the historical accuracy of the story, anything but what we're really thinking.

When the show is over, I help him take the dishes to the kitchen and stack them in the sink. Then, sitting side by side on the couch, we finish the wine and watch another episode. He doesn't make any move toward me, and whenever I look in his direction, his eyes are fixed on the screen. I want to reach out to him, to smooth away every sad memory, every fear I've evoked with my actions. I hate to see that I've hurt him, that I've reminded him of the type of emotions that ruined his parents' lives.

When the credits start to roll on the screen, I reach for his hand, my touch tentative. He turns to look at me, his eyes searching mine, and there's a stark vulnerability in his features that tugs at my heart.

"I'm sorry," I tell him again, my voice soft.

His fingers curl around mine, and something in his touch gives me hope that I haven't ruined something between us irreparably. "You don't have any reason to be jealous, Rachel. You have to believe me when I tell you that."

I nod. "I don't know what I was thinking," I say with a sigh. "I wasn't thinking at all."

"No matter what happens," he says, "don't run. I want this to work, and I want to be sure you want the same thing."

"I do," I tell him.

He nods and draws me closer to him. I lay my head on his chest, and one arm comes around me while the other hand strokes my hair. "I was so worried," he says, his voice low. "When your phone went off..." He sighs. "I don't think I've ever been so afraid in my life."

I close my eyes. I want to tell him then. *I love you Landon, and I was jealous because the thought of you with anyone else makes me feel like I'm dying.* But, I've become used to holding those words back. I sigh as he keeps stroking my hair, the sensations gently lulling me to sleep.

CHAPTER 12

*T*HE next day in the office, I go to the Swanson Court website to read about the opening gala. Landon has told me a little about it, and the information on the website confirms what I already know. There are some press events, then the main event, a fundraising gala for the Shelter Project.

I don't know much about that particular charity, so I follow a link to their website and read about the annual event, which is usually held in New York. It generally attracts some of the richest socialites, politicians, and Hollywood stars in the country. Now, they will all go to San Francisco to open the Gold Dust. It makes a lot of sense. Landon will get maximum publicity for his hotel, and the Shelter Project will get a substantial injection of funds from people with money to spend, people who can't afford not to be seen at such an event and those who are curious to see the changes to the hotel.

The same information about the gala from the Swanson Court website is presented on the Shelter Project site. The theme is A Midsummer Night's Dream, and the honorary chair of the event is Dane Riddell, a Hollywood heartthrob who recently broke hearts all over the world by getting married.

Wondering if there'll be someone else from Gilt Travel to write about the event, I look over the list of chairs for the event. The name of the editor of Gilt Style jumps out at me, along with another familiar name.

Ava Sinclair.

I frown, not sure if my suspicion is right. I remember a few weeks ago, that first time in San Francisco at the ballet event, Evans Sinclair's voice in my ear, hateful and angry. *He's been fucking her for years.* He was talking about Landon and his sister, the one who convinced his family to sell their hotel to Landon.

I don't know her name so I can't be sure she's the one.

But what if she is? It's no big deal if one of Landon's exes is involved in a charity event he is hosting. It doesn't mean anything. My mind goes back to the woman from the picture, but before I start to dwell on the thoughts, I push them out of my mind, replacing them with Landon's face from last night, how worried he was about me, the intensity with which he made love to me this morning.

I resist the urge to find out more about Ava Sinclair, and at lunchtime, I go out with Chelsea and Sonali. Sonali's skin is glowing from her cleanse, and she's mulling over an offer she got to intern with the New York branch of a European fashion house. She sulks prettily and expresses her indecision in her crisp British accent.

"I hear you guys are partying all night Friday," she says enviously. "I wish I could come, but I'm staying away from all my vices for a while, part of my cleanse."

"Oh!" I give her a sympathetic smile. "Well, I'm not partying all night, per se. I have to travel on Saturday."

Chelsea frowns. "Where?"

I tell them about Landon's opening night.

"Oh. I read about that." Chelsea says. "The world, their mother, and all the family diamonds are going to be there." She gives me a look. "What are you wearing?"

I shrug. "I haven't decided." I think of the card Landon gave me before we left his apartment. It was almost plain, embossed with the name of a store I'd never heard of. I knew of places like that, highbrow outfitters with direct contact with the best designers. I'd only have to call the number and I'd have something sublime to wear, paid for by Landon.

For some reason even I'm not sure of, I hesitate, thinking instead of getting Aunt Jacie to hook me up with one of her many fashion industry contacts. It's a sure way to get a couture dress at a great price.

Chelsea is looking at me as if I've gone insane. "You haven't..." She sighs. Sonali purses her lips, agreeing silently with whatever Chelsea is thinking. "I know what to do," Chelsea says, her eyes shining. "We'll go upstairs."

My eyes widen. 'Upstairs' is Gilt Style, and the legendary closet that holds decades worth of designer clothes and accessories, worth millions. "No!" I exclaim, not sure if it's even possible.

"Why ever not?" Even Sonali looks excited. "That place is a treasure trove."

"I have a friend up there," Chelsea declares with a wink. "Veronica Short, the head stylist who, lucky for you, owes me a favor." She leans forward with an excited grin. "She'll style you to within an inch of your life, Rachel. You'll love it."

"What kind of favor does she owe you?"

"Does it matter?" Chelsea grimaces. "What we

want is for you to look like a billion dollars, and she can make that happen."

That decides it. "Fine," I agree. "When?"

"I'll talk to her," Chelsea promises.

～

AFTER WORK, JOE IS THERE TO TAKE ME HOME. Laurie isn't back yet, so I'm left to prepare for Landon's cocktail mixer alone. By the time he arrives to pick me up, I'm all dressed up and ready. My dress is vintage Balenciaga, courtesy of my mom. It's a deep blue knee-length number with a neckline that's just low enough to reveal a hint of cleavage. My hair hangs down to my shoulders in loose waves, and my jewelry is simple—earrings and a matching bracelet.

When I open the door, Landon is standing there, devastatingly handsome in a black tux. His piercing gaze travels from my face to my dress and back up, and his eyes flare. "Rachel," he says simply, taking my hand. "I'll never get used to how beautiful you are."

And I will never get used to the pleasure of knowing that he sees me as beautiful. "Thank you," I reply, adding frankly, "You look fab, as usual." It will never be possible to be in the same room with him without being overcome by his perfection.

His hands trail down my arm, his fingers lingering

on my skin and making my body hum with pleasure. "Are you ready?"

"Yes," I murmur.

In the car, Landon's eyes continue to devour me, feeding a flowering of delight in my belly. "You look like you're about to jump my bones," I tell him.

"I'm trying not to." He laughs, the deep rumble making me smile with him. "We're leaving as early as we can manage. I'm not spending valuable time at a party when I'd rather be with you."

I run my tongue over my lower lip. "Now I don't want to go at all."

He pulls me onto his lap, careful not to wreck my clothes or my hair. "I'm going to have a hard time surviving two days without you," he murmurs. "What have you done to me?"

I raise a hand to smooth his silky hair. "I bewitched you," I reply, although I'm certain he's the one who's bewitched me.

He smiles. "You certainly did."

I close my eyes and lean my forehead on his, and we stay like that for a few moments. "Just so you know, I'll be having fun while you're gone." I give him a sly glance. "I'll be out clubbing all night Friday, so I won't miss you too much."

"So I'll be suffering alone." He sighs. "I think you just broke my heart."

I breathe, feeling a small heartache as I fill my lungs with air that's infused with *him*. "I'll miss you too," I tell him. "Every single minute."

There's a press line outside the venue of the party and we dutifully take pictures. Landon's hand never leaves the spot he has claimed around my waist as we walk inside together. Inside the venue, a champagne fountain refills glasses continuously, with different colored lights igniting the stacked flutes like muted rainbows.

Near the entrance, a tall, lanky man with a pleasant face and carefully side-swept brown hair breaks into a big grin when he sees Landon. They shake hands. The man is Steven Yeager, the host, and his smile widens when Landon introduces me as his girlfriend.

The statement causes a warmth to start somewhere in my chest and spread until I'm practically floating. I manage to compose myself and smile pleasantly at Steven. "Good to meet you," he says, giving me a conspiratorial look. "Hold on to him," he whispers, inclining his head toward Landon. "He's a big softie inside."

"I know," I respond, laughing. I look at Landon, and he's gazing at me with a smile. My heart tightens with the magnitude of my love for him, but the moment is broken by other people approaching him.

As the evening progresses, I smile and respond to introductions, all the while aware of Landon's hand around my waist, on the small of my back, his fingers gently stroking me through the fabric of my dress. I don't mind; I love his possessiveness, and I love his touch.

"Landon!"

The voice comes from behind us. It's a woman's voice, husky, rich, and almost certainly the voice of someone who is confident of the fact that she's beautiful.

We turn at the same time, Landon and I. Landon smiles at the new arrival while I take in the confirmation of all my suspicions from the sound of her voice. She is beautiful. Glossy black hair falls to her back and over her shoulders in soft waves, and perfect makeup enhances a face that's already classically beautiful. Her figure would be like a model's if not for the extra curviness that's shown off unapologetically in a sequined top, slim black pants, and classy heels.

I recognize her immediately—it's the woman from the picture, the woman Landon had dinner with when he told me he was working. I take a breath and keep the pleasant expression on my face, willing myself not to care, to remember Landon's assurance that there's nothing to be jealous about.

"Ava." Landon's hand slips from my waist as he steps forward to place a kiss on her cheek.

I feel the loss of that hand like the floor disappearing from under my feet. The woman is looking at me now, one eyebrow raised as she eyes me from my hair to my toes, her lips curled in a supercilious half-smile. Landon is introducing us, and I hear him say her name. Ava Sinclair.

He's been fucking her for years.

"How nice to meet you," she says. There is a mocking edge to her voice, barely perceptible, but there.

"It's good to meet you too," I reply pleasantly, although my mind is whirling. Landon was meeting with his ex? And even when I asked him, he conveniently neglected to tell me she was his former lover. He made it seem like I was jealous about just another business meeting with just another associate who happened to be female.

Meanwhile, it was someone he used to fuck.

It gives a whole new meaning to the way they smiled at each other in the picture, the hand she had on his arm.

I breathe. "I've met your brother," I tell her, intent on wiping the mocking smile from her face. "Evans Sinclair?" I smile wider. "It was a very...memorable meeting."

She blanches a little, but quickly recovers. So she's embarrassed by her brother? I hold her gaze and take a sip from my glass, and her eyes narrow slightly.

"I thought you'd returned to San Francisco," Landon says. He seems oblivious to the vibe I'm getting from her, or, I think sadly, maybe he just doesn't care.

"Not yet." She does a graceful headshake. "I had a few things to take care of." She gives me another look then turns to Landon with a dazzling smile. "I want to say hello to Steven," she says, taking his hand. "It's been ages. Why don't you come?"

She starts to move, then stops when he doesn't follow her. He's looking at me, and his eyes tell me he's not going anywhere without me. I decide to trust that and ignore the way Ava is holding on to his hand. It doesn't matter who she was to him, or what she wants now; that's none of my business. What matters is Landon, and the fact that right now, he's mine.

"We already saw him," I hear him tell her. She lets go of his hand and I feel a little triumph. She gives me a quick glance, but I respond with another pleasant smile. She smiles back, but it doesn't reach her eyes.

"All right then." She wiggles her fingers charmingly, giving Landon another bright smile before walking away.

We leave soon after that. On the way to his place, I decide not to ask him about her, or why he didn't think it was important to tell me she used to be his lover. I don't want to trigger any feelings of jealousy that I won't be able to contain, not tonight, not when he's leaving tomorrow. I don't want the night to end with us fighting.

If he knows the reason for my silence, he doesn't let on. As soon as the elevator deposits us in the foyer of his apartment, his lips are on mine, his hunger for me as real and tangible as the naked arousal pulsing through my body. We barely make it to his bedroom before he lifts my dress around my waist and bends me against the wall, ripping my panties and thrusting deep inside me.

He fucks me hard, his hands almost feverish as they explore my heated skin, but I don't care. I only care about my need to touch him, to feel him, to drive out the thoughts of him with anybody else.

By the time he makes me come over and over, again and again, and I finally fall asleep, sated and pliant, I've almost succeeded.

CHAPTER 13

*C*HELSEA comes through on the dress. A few hours after lunchtime, she leads me up to the Gilt Style floor, where everyone is insanely styled and so incredibly fashionable that they could all be models on a shoot. Nobody pays any attention to us as we make our way to the fashion department. There, we have to go up a flight of stairs to the storage floor, half of which houses the 'storage closet.'

The doors are already open, and Veronica Short, Chelsea's friend, is waiting. She's tiny, about five feet tall, with a shock of frizzy red hair. She drags on her e-cig and smiles at me. "You're Rachel?" She looks satisfied. "I love your coloring, and your hair is just perfect. It's A Midsummer Night's Dream? So a fairy-tale? I love it!"

At first, I feel like a culprit as she leads us into the closet, but the more she talks, the more I get infected with her excitement. We make our way through the vast storage space. It's totally crammed with unending closets, shoe racks, accessory bins... every usable space packed with something and labeled with code I don't even attempt to decipher. Veronica navigates it like she knows the location of every scarf and belt, unearthing dresses and shoes and hair accessories, making me try them on, clucking her disapproval with each one she doesn't like before tossing another one at me.

We finally settle on a pale blue dress from a current collection. It has a flattering neckline and a fitted bodice that hugs my waist and hips then flows down to drape loosely around my legs. The silky fabric at the neckline is studded with tiny glittering stones, which also rise from the hemline in exquisite patterns. Veronica smiles in approval and turns to Chelsea, who has been quiet since we came in. "What do you think?"

"It's fantastic," Chelsea says. She's leaning on one of the bins, nodding her head in approval. "It's perfect with your hair," she tells me. "You could pass for a wood nymph, or maybe Titania."

"Yeah right." I roll my eyes, but Veronica is nodding in agreement. She dashes off to find the right pair of shoes and a clutch then, sucking on her e-cig, she hurries off again. This time she returns with a box containing a large hair clip. She brushes my hair to one side and places the clip, then steps back and rubs her hand together.

"I think you're a genius, Veronica," Chelsea declares.

I shift a little so I can see my reflection in a visible part of the mirrored walls, and I gasp. I really do look like a wood nymph, something beautiful straight out of a fairytale.

"Wow!" I exclaim.

"I know." Veronica is grinning, and I feel so grateful I could hug her. She takes a picture with her phone then packs everything up in a box. "I'd better see your pictures somewhere that matters," she warns.

I'm going with Landon, so there's no way my picture won't end up somewhere that 'matters'—not that I really care. I have other things on my mind. Landon is already in San Francisco, probably caught in the whirl of final preparations and meetings, and somewhere in the same city is Ava Sinclair.

He's been fucking her for years.

I don't want to dwell on her, and I've tried not to,

but after I return to my office, my mind goes back to last night. They were comfortable with each other, friendly even. It didn't look as if she was nursing any rancor about Landon supposedly dropping her like a 'hot smelly potato' as her brother said.

Maybe Evans exaggerated, I tell myself. Maybe it was his imagination that Landon used his sister to get the Gold Dust. Maybe Landon and Ava were just friends and business partners. Maybe they were never lovers.

Even though I know the idea is wishful thinking, especially given her body language from last night, it still makes me feel better. I spend the next hour reading the comments on the latest of my articles on the Gilt Travel website, replying to just a few of them.

Joe is with Landon in San Francisco, so I have a replacement driver, Rafael. When I'm ready to go home, I call him, and by the time I get downstairs, he's waiting for me in a Swanson Court International town car. He's younger than Joe, Latino, with wistful brown eyes and hair in a long dark ponytail.

"Good evening," is all he says when I'm inside the car. Like Joe, he doesn't talk much.

"Good evening," I reply, wondering if reticence is a quality Landon looks for in employees. Just then, my phone starts to ring. It's Landon.

"Still at work?" His voice is deep and husky on the phone, and it reminds me of last night, that same voice whispering endearments in my ear while he made love to me.

I'm suddenly overcome by a wave of loneliness. "No. I'm on the way home."

"Lucky you." He sounds wistful.

"How are things?"

"We're ready." He pauses. "I'm mostly waiting for you to get here."

"What do you have planned for me?" I say with a smile.

I hear him chuckle. "Why don't you come and find out?"

I sigh, missing him so much it actually hurts.

"What are you thinking?" he asks.

"Just that I can't wait to see you either," I say truthfully.

"Rachel." He says my name slowly, almost as if he's savoring the sound on his tongue, and the knowledge that he feels the ache of our separation makes my heart swell. "Well, at least you still have your clubbing tomorrow night," he reminds me.

I manage a laugh. "You're still jealous."

He doesn't attempt to deny it. "I am, but I want you to have fun. I've arranged for Rafael to pick you up and take you wherever you want, in a car more suited to night crawling."

I raise a brow. "Really? What, a white stretch Cadillac limo?"

"Is that what you want?"

I sigh, knowing that if I said yes, he would make it happen. "Not particularly."

He chuckles. "Something less ostentatious," he says. "He'll also make sure you're safe."

This obsession with my safety...it's endearing, but tiring. "Why wouldn't I be safe?"

He doesn't reply. "I'll see you Saturday," he says. "I... Take care."

I...what? I release the breath I didn't realize I was holding. "Take care," I reply softly.

WE TALK AGAIN BEFORE I GO TO BED, AND THE next day on my way to work, and then again at lunchtime. After work, Laurie and I arrive early at Chelsea's place. She instructed us not to bother with hair and makeup, so when Rafael drops us at her Upper East Side apartment, we're still dressed casually.

A doorman lets us in from the street, then the receptionist checks to make sure that our names are on the visitor's list before directing us to an elevator.

"We should have let the parents pay for a place for us when they first offered," Laurie says in the elevator. "We could be living like this."

"Like, seriously," I agree, looking around the mirrored interior. Our parents tried to get us a place, but we were determined to be independent. They still paid the lease on our apartment, but it was closer to something Laurie and I could actually afford on our income without depending on them, or the money that somehow became ours when our dads sold a percentage of their business.

Chelsea's apartment is one of four on her floor. It isn't huge, but it's obviously expensive and professionally decorated. "Oh, you guys!" she exclaims, hugging Laurie and giving me one hurried air kiss. She has curlers in her hair and her nails are drying. "Come and get prettied up."

There are two stylists, Hector and Caesar. They're twins, and they are hilarious. Hector's eyelash extensions are longer than anyone, male or female, has a right to wear, and Caesar's leather pants are so tight, it's a wonder he can walk at all. They're from Bergdorf Goodman, so they know all the best gossip and keep it coming while they tweeze our brows, give us manicures, and fix our hair and makeup.

About two hours later, already in a good mood from the delicious chocolate liqueur Chelsea was very generous with, we troop downstairs, where Rafael is waiting in a classic black limo.

"I look like I need a pro footballer on my arm," Laurie says, catching her reflection in the tinted window glass. "What do you think?"

"Yup," I agree. She does look spectacular in a short black dress with studded platform heels. "They'd be lucky to be there."

"Awww." She smiles. "You're so wonderful."

Chelsea rolls her eyes and slides inside the car, scooting to the far side. "Come on girls, let's go. Tonight we're partying like rock stars."

The club we go to is called Felony. According to Chelsea, it's the newest and hottest in town. Once there, even though there's a queue as long as two blocks, she walks straight to the door, where the bouncer unclips the rope and lets us in.

Inside, the lights are dim, and the beat is strong enough to make my bones vibrate. The song playing is a very popular hip-hop jam, and my jaw almost drops when I see that the singer, a hip-hop phenomenon, is actually performing it on a raised stage.

"Cool, right?" A blue strobe light hits Chelsea's face, showing her broad grin.

I have to scream over the music. "Hell yes!"

"Come on." She grabs my hand. "The bar's over there."

We order shots and down two each. The burning sensation shoots straight from my throat and stomach to my head. Beside me, Laurie is nodding her head to the music.

"I need another drink, then I'm hitting the floor." She looks at me. "Game?"

I nod. "Of course."

We order two more shots. Chelsea is being chatted up by a sexy guy with a heavily muscled chest showed off in a tight t-shirt. He looks vaguely familiar, and I realize I've seen him on TV, in a popular sitcom. I look around, wondering how many famous people are among the gyrating bodies on the dance floor.

I'm about to tell Laurie I'm ready to dance when strong arms encircle me from behind. Spinning around, I come face to face with Chadwick Black.

"Chadwick!" I return his hug. "What're you doing here?"

"What are *you* doing here?" he throws back. I haven't seen him since the day I ran into him at the office, and I had no idea he was still in town. "You look fabulous," he says, looking me over. "Absolutely delicious."

I roll my eyes. "Are you stalking me now?"

He grins. "Maybe. Where's your delightful cousin?"

"Ha!" I laugh, wagging a finger in his face. "Like I'm going to tell you."

Laurie has been talking to Chelsea, and she chooses that moment to turn back toward me. She sees Chadwick and her face lights up with a delighted smile. "Hi, Chadwick Black."

"Hi," he drawls before turning back to give me a triumphant grin. "You and I are going to dance all night."

She gives him a coy smile. "Can you keep up?"

"Try me."

She shrugs. "Maybe later. I'm dancing with Rachel."

"Please go on," I tell her, sure she'll have more fun dancing with Chad. "I'll just have another drink."

She gives me a questioning glance then follows Chad, who looks grateful, and I watch them disappear into the crowd on the dance floor. Chelsea ditches her sitcom actor and joins me. Two cute guys offer to buy us drinks and we let them, then we abandon them at the bar to join Laurie and Chadwick on the floor. We start out dancing together, but I soon find myself dancing with some guy, then a girl with startling blue hair and a lip piercing, then another guy. The music stays good and I hardly notice as time flies.

I return to the bar after a while, and some time later, Laurie comes to join me. Her eyes are bright, and there's a slight sheen on her skin from all the dancing. "What's up?"

"Nothing." I shrug. "Where's Chad?"

"Bathroom." She props her hip on a stool. "He's cool."

"He's still a whore," I whisper, wrinkling my nose.

She laughs. "He's leaving for a party at the Insomnia Lounge, wants to know if we'll come."

I raise my brows and she shrugs. The Insomnia is Landon's club, and she knows. Of course I want to go there. I smile, remembering the last time, Landon appearing like a figure out of my fantasies, hypnotizing me with his eyes and his touch until I would gladly have followed him anywhere. He was playing a game that night, trying to see if I would confess that I wasn't the hooker I'd made him think I was.

"I'll ask Chelsea," I tell Laurie.

Chelsea is eager to go, and we pile into the limo for the drive to the Insomnia Lounge. The line there is even longer, and this time, we don't have a pass, but Chadwick's host has left his name at the door, and we get to saunter in like VIPs again.

The music is alive. There are dancers hanging

from the ceiling doing impossible acrobatics, and on the dance floor, people are moving to the sexy music. The party Chadwick came to join is taking place in a private glass-walled room beyond the VIP area. It's an eclectic mix of people, including a famous rock musician, two NBA players, a writer for the New York times, a ballerina, an actor, and another photographer. I recognize some of Chadwick's artists friends and a couple of groupies of the hot female variety.

Everybody seems happy to see Chadwick, and we join the party seamlessly. The focus of the group appears to be the rock musician who's celebrating something I don't quite hear. Chelsea starts to flirt with him, and he looks like he can't believe his luck.

Drinks are flowing, and Laurie and Chadwick are still engrossed in each other enough to make me worry for Brett. A guy seated beside me starts a conversation. He's a sports lawyer, very confident too. He starts telling me about all the high-profile players he represents, and I'm actually relieved when he excuses himself to go to the bathroom.

A few moments later, someone else takes his seat.

"Hi Rachel," the new arrival says, in a familiar voice that makes me jump in surprise.

"Jack!" I breathe, surprised to see him.

"Yup." His eyes flick over my body. "You look beautiful."

"Thanks," I reply. "You look good too." He really does. His hair is tousled, and he's slowing joining the beard gang, sporting a small overgrowth, while his expensive sweater and slim-fitted jeans make him look casual and cool.

He nods and looks around the room before looking back at me. "You know Jem?"

He's talking about the rocker. I shake my head. "No. I was out with Chelsea and Laurie and kinda ended up here."

"Ah!" He chuckles. He holds my gaze for a long moment before I look away, remembering our last awkward conversation. "So, where's the boyfriend?" I hear him ask.

"He's in San Francisco," I reply.

"For the big opening," Jack says. "Why aren't you with him? I was already getting used to seeing the photographs of you on his arm."

It's not like him to be snide, and I search his face, a frown on mine. He doesn't look as if he knows that he's being rude. "I didn't realize you'd started reading gossip blogs," I respond. "But don't give up on the photographs just yet. I'm joining him tomorrow."

"Whoa." He laughs, but it doesn't reach his eyes. "Don't be so combative. I just asked a question." When I don't reply, he sighs. "You've changed, Rachel."

I give him a short laugh. "I sure hope so."

A new song starts to play. I watch as Chelsea pulls the rocker to his feet and they start dancing.

"Wanna dance?" Jack asks.

I shake my head. "I've danced enough for one night."

We're both silent after that, but I'm aware of him beside me. I wonder what he's thinking, and if he still believes that Landon doesn't deserve me. I feel his eyes on me, and I turn toward him. He has a sad and thoughtful expression on his face.

"What?" I ask gently, unnerved by the depth of emotions in his eyes.

He keeps looking at me, his eyes searching my face. "Are you happy?" he asks finally.

There is a false sense of intimacy created by how close we're sitting, by the familiarity of his features, by the knowledge that he knows me better than most people. For a moment, I'm tempted to open up to him, to tell him my fears about Landon, but I hold back, choosing not to respond to the question. Am I happy? Yes, when I'm with Landon. When I don't have to think of anything else but the fact that he's with me, I'm content, but when I allow myself to think of what we are, of where we're going...

Jack is watching my face, as if he's reading my emotions on my features. I look away from his searching eyes, and at that moment, a couple enters the room. The man is the sports lawyer who was flirting with me earlier. The woman looks slightly older, with straightened blonde hair and a nice figure. She waves at Jack then comes over to say hi, leaving her companion to find them seats.

"Sweetheart," she coos, kissing his cheeks.

"This is Cecily," he tells me after their greeting. "Cecily, Rachel."

The woman peers at me as if I look familiar to her. "Hello," she says.

"You two have Landon Court in common," Jack says. He lounges back on his seat. "Cecily lasted about three months, am I right?"

Cecily's face clouds then she shrugs before giving me a speculative look. "You're the new girl-friend," she says. "I thought I'd seen your face somewhere." Her companion signals to her from across the room and she starts to leave, but then turns back to me. "Word of advice? Don't ask him about the future."

She's gone before I say what's on the tip of my tongue—that I don't need her advice.

"What is wrong with you?" I hiss at Jack. "You're parading Landon's exes just to prove something to me?"

"The opportunity presented itself," he says with a

shrug at my annoyed expression. "I care about you, Rachel."

"Oh please!" I toss at him, getting up. "I'm obviously not the only one who's changed, Jack. I don't remember you being this much of an asshole." I stalk out of the room, heading downstairs to the bathroom. I waste time in there, reapplying my lip gloss and staring at my reflection in the mirror.

Don't ask him about the future.

He's been fucking her for years.

I'm trying, *really* trying not to entertain my fears about my relationship with Landon. I'm trying to exist contentedly in the knowledge that at least he wants to be with me too, that for now at least, he needs me as much as I need him.

But it's so hard when every minute something comes up to remind me of the heartache that is surely going to be part of my future with him.

I try to dismiss Jack and his friend, try to shrug off what she said, and then I see Ava Sinclair's face in my head. She's in San Francisco right now, with him. I close my eyes as insane possibilities assault my mind, until it feels like I can't breathe.

My phone is in my purse. I retrieve it and type her name in the search panel. I don't know exactly what I'm looking for, but my greatest dread is that I'll find something to confirm my fears.

The first result is a news article from yesterday evening. I click on it. *"The brightest and the most beautiful!"* the headline screams, then there's a picture of Landon walking out of a building with Ava Sinclair.

He may be taking over the hotel that has been in her family for generations, but it seems that it's Ava Sinclair who has billionaire Landon Court wrapped around her little finger. The twice-divorced socialite was spotted with the hotelier at the Fairmont Royal in San Francisco after enjoying a cozy dinner. Sources say they have a passionate history. Is this old romance being rekindled?

I study the picture, trying to read everything about their body language and the self-satisfied smirk on her face. It doesn't help that she looks exquisite even in a candid picture.

He's been fucking her for years.

What is she to Landon exactly? Why is he spending so much time with her?

I type a quick text to Rafael letting him know I'm ready to leave. Then I send one to Laurie, telling her I have a headache and Rafael will be back to pick up her and Chelsea whenever they're ready to go home. There's a crush of people on the way to the exit, and I push past them, willing myself to stop thinking.

SERENA GREY

You decided to be with him for as long as you could, I tell myself. Don't overthink anything.

I repeat it as a mantra in my head until I make it outside. There's still a line of people trying to get in, and I can't see Rafael yet. As I wait, I search my mind for all the reassuring things Landon has ever said to me, everything that makes me sure, deep down, that we have something that's more than just sex.

Then I see Ava Sinclair's smirk, and I forget how to think.

"Rachel."

Jack is walking up to me. He looks as if he ran out after me, but I don't care what he wants. I blame him for ruining my evening, and my peace of mind.

"What?" I hiss at him. "What do you want?"

He sighs. "I'm sorry about back there. I just wanted to show you what kind of man—"

"Oh fuck you, Jack!" I say it loud enough that a few people turn to look at us. "You can't stand to lose your favorite toy, is that it? You can't stand that I've moved on? For God's sake, Jack! Get over it."

"I can't." He closes the distance between us, and there's an intensity in his eyes I never saw there in all the time we were together. "I can't. Rachel, I...I love you okay? I'm in love with you."

I close my eyes, all the anger slowly draining out of me, replaced by confusion and sadness. My first

244

thought is of everything I would give to have Landon be the one standing in front of me and saying those words.

Maybe Jack takes my silence as capitulation because he steps forward and takes my face in his hands, kissing me with something that feels like desperation.

It only lasts for a few seconds. I push away from him just as I see Rafael parking the limo and stepping out, his eyes on Jack.

"Are you all right?" he asks me, rushing over to insert himself between me and Jack.

"Yes, I'm fine." I spare a glance at Jack, hoping that the displeasure in my eyes is enough to communicate that there is never going to be another chance for him, and then I follow Rafael to the waiting car.

CHAPTER 14

$\mathcal{L}$AURIE is asleep when I leave for the airport. I was still awake and thinking about Landon when she came in at about three in the morning. I had planned to ask her how it went with Chadwick, but I can do that over the phone.

I spend the hours on the plane trying to read, but my thoughts keep intruding, my mind traveling to some imagined future where Landon is no longer a part of my life. I imagine the emptiness, the desolation, and it feels so real...

...and inevitable.

Then there's Jack, and his declaration of love. Love! What the fuck was he thinking?

I give up on reading and bury my face in my hands. I see Jack in my memories, the way I used to see him all those months when I hung on to him, thinking he was the man for me. Then I remember his petty attack on Landon last night, and that unwanted kiss. It makes me so angry that I wish I never had to see him again.

He's never been the man for me. Maybe if he'd been the man I needed him to be from the start, I'd never have met Landon. If he hadn't rejected me when I told him I loved him, maybe we'd still be together, maybe I'd be happy, satisfied that I had everything I wanted.

The picture is as lackluster as is usual with all my attempts to imagine my life without Landon. It's as if he has defined what happiness is for me, what satisfaction is, and yet...

I hear Jack's voice clearly inside my head.

Are you happy?

Am I?

I allow myself to concentrate on the fact that Landon is waiting for me, taking pleasure from the thought. At the airport, an unfamiliar driver picks me up for the journey to the Gold Dust.

My phone buzzes just as the car starts to move. It's Landon.

Tell me you've arrived.

I have.

I can't wait to see you.

My belly contracts. I know what he means. When I think of being in the same space with him, touching him, every other thought disappears.

Me neither.

Soon we're at the Gold Dust, and as we approach, I realize my error in thinking the hotel was close to completion the last time I was here. In just a month, so much more has been done. A fountain is spouting near the entrance, the sound of the water muted and almost hypnotic. Blooming shrubs line the path to the main doors, where two uniformed doormen are stationed even though the doors slide open mechanically as soon as I approach.

Inside, the lobby seems to be gleaming, with shiny walls and floor, beautiful furniture, luscious plants, and creative light fixtures. I'm barely inside before a familiar face approaches me—Tony, Landon's assistant.

"Miss Foster, welcome to the Gold Dust. I trust you enjoyed your flight."

"Yes, I did." I'm a little disappointed, as if a part of me had been expecting Landon to be waiting for me instead of his assistant. I smile at Tony as a bellboy wheels my luggage in from the trunk of the car. "It was smooth. How are the preparations?"

"Fine." He grins. "Actually, it's kind of crazy," he continues with a small laugh. "But that's okay. If there's anything else you need...? Mr. Devin will be here any moment to take you to your suite, but anything else, let me know."

I shake my head. He looks like he has a lot on his plate. "I'll be okay. Don't worry about me."

He smiles. "Then I wouldn't be doing my job."

I see Claude approaching us. The Frenchman breaks into a broad grin. "Welcome back, Miss Foster!" His accent is a delight as always.

"Everything looks lovely," I tell him as Tony takes his leave. "How is it going?"

Claude gives an exaggerated shrug. "What can I say? It is a delight to see your lovely face."

He starts to lead me toward the elevators and I follow him, looking around. "I'm sure things are hectic."

"Insane," he agrees with a nod. "But Mr. Court is here, so he solves problems as soon as they occur. He has instructed that I attend to your every need, so let me know if there's anything you require."

"Nothing at the moment."

He nods as the elevator opens directly into one of the penthouse suites. Claude stays to give directions to the bellboy while I go to the balcony to admire the view.

"Would you like lunch sent up?" Claude is hovering.

"No." I already ate something light on the plane. "Don't worry about me, I'm sure you have a lot to do."

He nods and leaves me. I fetch myself a glass of juice from the kitchen, and when I return to the balcony, my phone is ringing. It's Landon again.

"Are you settled in?"

"Yes." I smile. "The hotel is beautiful, Landon."

He sighs. "I'm glad you think so."

"Where are you?" I ask.

"Downstairs." He pauses. "Do you have everything you need?"

"Yes!" I laugh. "Everybody keeps asking me that."

I hear him breathe. "I want to see you," he says. "I have the press conference in about half an hour. After that, I'm coming to you."

"Are you sure you have the time?" I ask, even though I want nothing more than to see him.

"I'll make it," he says determinedly. "I'm so fucking hot for you." I pull in a breath, instantly responding to his desire. He's not done. "I'm going to fuck you so hard, you'll feel it for days."

My body clenches in arousal. "You have a hotel to open," I tease, breathless, "and homeless people to raise money for. Are you sure you should be thinking about sex at a time like this?"

"Can you blame me?" He laughs. "I have a hard-on

just from the knowledge that you're here, and it's not going anywhere until you take me inside your hot, delicious pussy."

A small moan escapes my lips. I love it when he talks like that, about the things he plans to do to me. "You're making me so hot."

"Stay that way. I'll be with you as soon as I can manage it."

When our conversation is over, I go to the main bedroom in the suite. My things have been unpacked in the walk-in closet, beside Landon's clothes. In the bathroom, his brands of toiletries are placed alongside mine. I freshen up, loving the feeling that our lives are intersected, that we're a real couple.

Back in the living room, I switch on the TV and flip through the channels. I doze off while listening to the local news then wake up when I hear Landon's voice.

I see his face on the TV. He's answering a question, his self-assurance and confidence, coupled with his fierce masculine beauty, hypnotic to watch.

Most of the questions are expected. *How does it feel to add a new hotel to your brand?* Etc., etc. Landon replies cheerfully, inserting a joke here and there, deftly putting everyone at ease.

"How are you dealing with the rumors about your unlawful acquisition of property?"

The question is followed by silence, and I see Landon pause, his eyes measuring the reporter who asked, an older woman, nondescript in a brown suit.

He smiles easily before he starts to reply. The smile assures me—and I suspect most of the people in the room with him—that he has nothing to worry about, and neither do they. "I should clarify that the rumors are not about the unlawful acquisition of property. They are merely speculation, driven by gossip, about the reasons why people feel confident enough to entrust their properties to the Swanson Court brand. If you take a look at the Gold Dust today Miss..."

"Hader."

"Miss Hader." He pauses. "Compared to the Gold Dust of say, two years ago, the reason should be obvious."

More questions follow after that. I remember the article I read...what had it talked about? Use of coercion. Landon told me about having difficulty in purchasing a property in Europe. He'd spent an afternoon convincing the seller, who'd suddenly changed her mind about selling to him. Why? Could it have been the rumors? Who would hate him enough to spread such stories?

My mind goes to Evans Sinclair. His board had made him sell his hotel to Landon, and apparently he thought that was a good reason to hate him. Could he be the one feeding the rumors?

My eyes go back to Landon on the screen, watching his calm demeanor. How far would he go if he really wanted something? Far enough to stretch the boundaries of the law? Did 'convincing' mean the same thing to him as it did to other people? Would he put them in a position where they couldn't, or didn't want to say no, like he did with me?

I shake my head. Landon isn't a bully. He is the kind of man who identifies opportunities and follows them. He shows people the advantages of working with him, rather than bending them forcefully to his will.

At that moment, he walks into the suite. It's strange, seeing him on TV and in the room at the same time. He's looking at something on his phone, a frown on his face. He looks up at me, an indecipherable expression on his face.

"Hey." I smile at him.

He shoves the phone into his pocket and looks at the TV screen. "I hate press conferences," he says, shaking his head.

"You handled that one well enough."

"I had to."

"I read about the rumors," I tell him, ashamed

now that I forgot and instead chose to concentrate on the picture of him with Ava. "Is it a problem?"

"Not really." He shrugs. "I know who's behind them, and he's bound by contract not to slander me directly, so he's planting the gossip with the help of his social circle. They have gotten out of hand, but they only damage public perception. The banks and investors don't care. Most businesspeople would rather cut off their ears than stop doing business with me."

His confidence reassures me. He shrugs off his jacket and tosses it on one of the chairs. Then, instead of joining me on the couch, he goes over to the glass walls, loosening his tie as he walks. He looks out at the spectacular view, which stretches from the balcony outside to the bay and the horizon beyond. It's majestic, but nowhere near as perfect as him.

I get up to join him, drawn to him as if by a magnet. He turns to me, his hand rising to linger on my check.

"Are you worried?" I ask.

"No." He shakes his head. "Have you had anything to eat?"

"I'm not hungry," I whisper, leaning into his hand. "Not for food anyway."

He sighs, his eyes sliding away from mine. Is he keeping something from me? My fears rear their ugly heads again but disappear when he takes my face between his hands and rests his forehead on mine. The gesture is unexpectedly tender, and I close my eyes.

I love you.

As if he heard the thought in my mind, he draws in a breath and releases my face, pulling off his tie and tossing it in the direction of the couch. Then he reaches for me, one hand curving around the back of my neck to pull me in for a kiss. It's a soft one, light and sweet, making my body quiver as his tongue gently tastes my lips.

I sigh, and he leans back to study me for a moment. Frowning, I reach for him, placing my hands on his chest and feeling his warm, hard body beneath. I've missed him, his body, his touch...it has been two long days after all.

"You said something about fucking me so hard I would feel it for days."

He tilts his head slightly, his eyes still on mine. "Yes, I remember."

I frown, wondering what he's waiting for. I trail my hand down his chest, over the hard board of his stomach, down the front of his pants, feeling his erection, a thick pressure against my palm. I drop a kiss on his still clothed chest. "I'm so ready," I whisper.

I sense his hesitation again, but before I can truly let myself wonder why, it's gone. His hand snakes around me, lifting me against his body while he moves. I feel the glass wall at my back just as his lips cover mine again.

This time, the kiss is deep and demanding. His tongue strokes mine, sending sweet hot shivers coursing through me. I kiss him back, sucking on his lips, his tongue. He lowers his hands to stroke my thighs, lifting my dress as his hands travel back up to my waist. Still kissing me, he molds the curve of my ass then slips one hand into the crotch of my panties.

His fingers slide over the heated center of my arousal, and his teeth graze my lower lip. "You're so wet."

"I told you I was ready," I reply breathlessly.

He takes hold of the hem of my dress and pulls it over my head. Then he lowers his head to bite my nipple through my bra, making me squirm. I bury one hand in his silky hair, the other greedily stroking the swollen evidence of his need for me.

He groans and lifts his face from my breasts, and his heated lips settle on mine again. I undo his belt and button fly, sliding my hand inside his briefs to feel the warm heat of his throbbing cock.

Touching him makes me moan against his lips. I push him back and drop to my knees, pulling his briefs down to his thighs so I can take him in my mouth. He's hot and hard, and I suck him greedily, feeling the wetness of my arousal dripping down my swollen sex.

I stroke my tongue along the underside of his cock and hear him growl, pulling out of my mouth to join me on the floor. He rests on his haunches before lowering my head back to his cock. I sigh and take him in again, hollowing my cheeks, sucking him deep, loving the taste of his skin and the feel of him against my lips and tongue.

He rocks his hips, grinding into my mouth, the sound of pleasure he makes getting me hotter and even more aroused. His hands move feverishly over my back, stroking my skin, and he leans over me to slide them into my panties and cup and squeeze my butt cheeks. I spread my legs so he can slide his fingers into me from behind and stroke the heat of my dripping center.

"I love your mouth," he whispers, kissing the skin of my back and grazing his teeth across my skin. "So hot..."

I moan in response with his cock still in my mouth. He sighs and leans back upright, his hands coming up along my back to thread in my hair. "I want to come inside you," he says, pulling out and pushing me up to my feet. Still kneeling, he pulls down my panties, pressing his lips between my legs, nuzzling me and sucking on my clit.

Sensation spreads through me and I grind against his lips, moaning his name. He slips his fingers inside me, and my body clenches around them. With a growl, he gets to his feet and steers me toward the wall, stopping when my back is pressed against the glass. Then he lifts me off the floor, spreading my thighs and pressing the tip of his cock against me.

I wrap my legs around his waist, urging him inside. He obliges me, ramming into me so deep that my back rubs against the wall. I brace my hands on his shoulders and he lets go of my thighs, his hands coming up to pull down the top of my bra and expose my heavy swollen breasts and sensitive nipples.

His lips part, and he makes a rough sound in his throat. He braces one hand behind me and lowers the other to plump one aching breast, then he lowers his head to suck hard on the other nipple as he starts to pump into me.

My toes curl. The pleasure is beyond intense. He fucks me like a starving man, as if he wants to leave a mark on me, and I love every minute of it. I moan my pleasure, whispering in his ear, telling him how good it feels, how I want him to fuck me forever.

His thrusts grow faster, more feral. I tighten my legs around him, my body curling with intense pleasure. Waves of sensation wash over me, and I come, crying out his name.

Still hard, he pulls out of me then drops me to my unsteady legs and turns me around so I'm facing the wall. I barely have time to brace my hands on the glass before he pushes into me again. Sensation fills me, and I cry out weakly. The pleasure intensifies as he starts to move, each deep thrust giving me everything I need and more.

His hands flex at my hips, rubbing feverishly over my heated skin. He bends over me, pressing his chest against my back as his hands come around me to squeeze my breasts. He rubs my tender nipples, making me cry out in pleasure as he strokes me deep inside with the sweet thrusts of his cock.

"Don't stop," I beg, even though I know he won't. Blood rushes through me. Through the glass I can see the view outside, the other buildings, and I know no one can see us, but there's an abandoned sense of exhibition at the thought that they might. I tighten my body around Landon, my inner muscles gripping him tightly. He growls and thrusts harder, each strong flexing of his hips making me forget everything, everything but him and how unbelievably good he feels inside me.

"I'm going to come." He breathes harshly, one

hand releasing my breast to rub hard at my clit. "You're going to make me come so hard."

I lose my breath, my hands pushing on the glass as my body goes weak. A river of heat explodes between my thighs, spreading through me, and I cry out helplessly as my body clenches violently around his cock. He fucks me through my loud climax, riding it to his own. When he comes, he breathes my name, his muscles tensing as the warm spurts of his orgasm add to the pleasurable heat inside me.

He sags against my body, his chest covering the sweat-sheened skin of my back. After a few seconds, he pulls out of me and turns me to face him so he can press kisses all over my face. I wrap my arms around him, feeling incredibly close to him.

"You really did miss me," I tease, breathless.

"You haven't seen anything yet," he replies. He chuckles and adjusts my bra then picks up my dress and panties and hands them to me. He adjusts his own clothes before dropping another kiss on my lips.

"I can't wait," I say, laughing, before adding seriously, "I missed you so much."

His smile disappears, and his eyes search my face. I frown, sensing the same hesitation from before.

"What's the matter?" I ask softly, the vibe I'm getting from him bringing my own fears to my mind. "Is something wrong?"

"You should get dressed," he says, his eyes flicking to the dress I'm still holding. "There's nothing wrong."

He's obviously deflecting. My shoulders drop, my mind going back to last night, that picture of him and Ava Sinclair. "Tell me what's wrong."

At first I think he's going to deflect again, but then he raises a hand to cup my chin. "I don't like to share what's mine," he says, a dark edge to his voice. "Not now, not ever. Do you understand?"

I step back, suddenly aware that I'm only wearing a bra. I clutch my dress, feeling naked. "What are you talking about?"

"I'm talking about Jack Weyland."

I meet his gaze, realizing as I see the expression on his face that he knows about last night, about the kiss. My face creases in a frown as the high from my orgasm dissipates.

"Is that why you have Rafael driving me around?" I ask evenly. "So you can spy on me?"

"I didn't need to spy on you. You kissed him in front of my club. I didn't need Rafael to tell me about that."

He couldn't have known when we spoke earlier. I remember the expression on his face when he walked into the suite, reading something on his phone. He'd probably found out just then.

"You could have asked me what happened instead of jumping to conclusions," I say softly.

"Oh?" He raises his eyebrows. "Really?"

"Yes, really." I glare at him. "For your information, he kissed me. I neither wanted it nor invited it, and you know what? I don't like to share what's mine either, so the next time you decide to enjoy Ava Sinclair's company, you can keep that in mind."

I leave him standing there and stalk to the bedroom. What right did he have to police my actions? I tried to swallow my jealousy about Ava because I didn't want to accuse him unnecessarily, and his first reaction to an unwanted, uninvited kiss was to accuse me.

Still clutching my dress, I go to the bathroom door and start to open it, but Landon's voice stops me.

"I thought we had this conversation about Ava," he says, his voice low.

"I thought we had the conversation about Jack," I toss back. "Why were you with her yesterday? Why didn't you tell me you used to sleep with her when I saw that picture of you two?"

"I've never asked you for an inventory of everyone you ever slept with," Landon replies. "Do you think I should punctuate everything I say about her with a statement about how, a long time ago, we used to fuck?"

I pull in a short breath. So that part was true. "Maybe it would have been fair for you to give me that information seeing as everywhere I look, the two of you are being photographed together. Was it also a business meeting yesterday?" I say mockingly. "Did you decide to 'save time' by concluding your business over dinner?"

He laughs bitterly. "You're one to talk. I'm supposed to endure an inquisition whenever you see and totally misconstrue a picture. Meanwhile, it's perfectly okay for you to spend as much time as you like with your precious Jack."

"My precious Jack?" I shake my head. I'm so angry, I want to scream in frustration, to cry, or break something. I close my eyes and sigh tiredly. "You know what? I have no idea why we're arguing. We both know why we're still together, so we might as well forget the things we can't agree about and you know, maybe fuck... That's obviously the only area where we work well together."

His jaw sets, and I turn away from him, opening the door to the bathroom. I don't see him start to move until he reaches me. "You're right," he says, taking my arm and pulling me around. "Maybe we should do just that."

I pull my arm away from his grip. "Just as long as you know I'm not Ava."

His laugh is angry and derisive. "And you know I'm not Jack."

I'm suddenly on the verge of tears. "God! How can you be so—"

"So what?" he interrupts. "So jealous? But you know exactly how that feels don't you?" One hand is at my waist pulling me to him while the other pushes between my legs. "This is mine," he says. "You are mine"—he slides his fingers through the wetness in my core—"and your body knows it."

I'm ashamed of the pleasure I feel when he touches me. I'm ashamed of how my anger ceases to matter. I should push him away, tell him to go to hell, but his fingers slide into me and I moan his name. "Landon..." I'm not sure if I want to ask him to stop, or to shut up and fuck me.

"It's what you want isn't it? It's the only reason you ever agreed to be with me." He lifts me off my feet and carries me to the bed, laying me on my back, my legs spread. "You like how it feels when my cock is deep inside you. That's what you want."

He kneels between my legs, quickly undoing his pants and freeing his cock. He's hard again, his face set. There is no tenderness in what he's about to do, just pain, jealousy, and anger.

I should correct him, I should tell him I'm here because I want to be with him, because I love him.

But I don't. I can't. It's the last shield I have to protect my heart, so I concentrate on how much I want him, because even though he's the source of the ache in my heart, he's also the only one who can take it away. He's like a drug—bad for me in the long run, but the only thing that can make me feel good right now.

"Yes," I whisper. "It's what I want."

He plunges into my tight core with a deep grunt. He's hard and hot, and his thrusts are deep and fast, as if he's working out his feelings by fucking me. My fingers twist in the sheets, all my anger, all my fury coalescing into a need to take what I can from him, to enjoy the pleasure without regret, and it brings me swiftly to a rolling climax.

It's over quickly for him too. He rolls off me, lying on his back beside me, his breaths coming fast.

I start to get up, but he sits up and reaches for my hand, pulling me back gently to sit beside him. He keeps my hand in his, his fingers wrapping around mine in a way that would feel tender and protective if I wasn't so sad. "I should have told you about Ava," he whispers. "I'm sorry. I didn't think it mattered. I was wrong."

I raise one shoulder in a small shrug. "It's okay."

There is a short silence. "I tried not to care about you and Jack," he says. "You told me you no longer have feelings for him, and I tried to concentrate on that. I...I just couldn't."

The same way I've been trying not to care about Ava. I swallow. "I know how the kiss with Jack would have seemed to you, but it wasn't what it looked like."

He lets go of my hand as I get to my feet. His body is hunched over, and I want to reach for him, to hold him maybe, to recapture the feeling of closeness we had a few hours ago.

But I don't. I leave him sitting there and go to the bathroom to take a shower.

CHAPTER 15

*A*FTERWARD, we eat in silence. I've showered and changed into casual pants and a top. He has also changed into a black long-sleeved tee and light gray pants. It's testament to how sad I am that I can't even concentrate on how devastatingly appealing he looks.

We really have nothing to build a relationship on, I see that now—just sex, and the things we keep from each other. What kind of relationship can we have if we don't trust each other, if the moments of happiness and intimacy are so soon followed by accusations and pain?

Landon's brow is furrowed. He looks as troubled as I'm feeling. Our eyes meet, and the helpless somberness in his gaze makes me want to cry. "The gala starts at eight," he tells me, his voice low.

"I know," I reply, my own voice small.

"Claude will provide anything you need, hair, makeup, whatever. He's already been instructed."

I don't reply.

I can feel his eyes on my face. "Aidan will be here. He's landing in the evening."

That brings a small smile to my lips. "I'd like to see him," I say. "What about Jules and Cameron?" I enjoyed the company of his friend Cameron McDaniel and his heavily pregnant wife during my last visit. "Will they come?"

He smiles. "They can't make it. Jules is expecting any minute."

I chuckle. "Of course."

The small talk dries out after that, and after we eat, Landon leaves the suite, going back downstairs to conclude preparations for tonight.

If trying to act like everything was okay had been a drain, being alone is worse.

Are you happy? Jack's voice whispers in my head.

I am not. The weight of all my chaotic emotions from the past few weeks feels so heavy now. How could I have thought I could bear it? I feel like I'm breaking into pieces, unsure where the real source of my pain is.

He'll never love me.

One day, when he finds out how I really feel about him, he'll recoil from the idea of returning my love, and he'll walk away.

My insecurities about our relationship will continue to eat me alive until that day comes.

No, I'm not happy.

The thoughts chase through my mind until I want to scream.

How did we end up here? Neither of us really knew what it meant, this 'relationship' we agreed to have. We didn't define anything, no boundaries, no feelings, just sex, jealousy, and allusions, but never the truth.

I should have told you about Ava, he'd said. Told me what exactly? Only that they used to be lovers? He didn't bother to explain why he was suddenly spending so much time with her. Was last night's picture also of a work meeting? It's no use wondering, and I know I won't ask him now—what would be the point?

My phone is on the couch beside me, and almost as if I have a masochistic desire to punish myself, I go back to the article from last night, to look at the picture of Landon and Ava.

Sources say they have a passionate history, I read again, wondering what exactly happened between them. *I just want to know for sure,* I tell myself as I type in a search term with both their names.

The results are few and span a period of years. There's a small sound bite about a house party in the Hamptons from about seven years ago, where they are referred to as 'scions of hotel dynasties' and described as an item. Then there's a report from a year later about her marriage to an Italian racecar driver from an immensely wealthy family.

A gossip item puts them together again about three years later; they're sailing in Europe after her divorce. A followup article claims she has broken his heart and is dating a tech billionaire, then in another one dated soon after, they're together again, having dinner in New York.

It goes on like that, and I start to wonder if I'm just another temporary separation, like her marriages. The thought is heartbreaking. I close my browser, set the phone on the table, and close my eyes, covering my face with my hands.

I'm not going to think about Ava, I decide. She's not even the problem. Even if she hadn't appeared, Landon and I would still have arrived here, at this point, where the only sensible thing was to accept that we just weren't working.

It's clear what I should do, but when I remember

how numb I was without him, I don't know if I have the strength.

I hear my phone ringing, and I almost decide not to take the call, but I change my mind when I see that it's Laurie.

"Helloooo." She draws out the word, sounding cheerful. In the back of my mind, I wonder if Chadwick has anything to do with that. "How's Frisco?"

"Great." I try to sound upbeat. "How are you?

"I'm lovely. Going on a date tonight, actually."

"With Chadwick?"

"Yes." She sighs. "He's making me dinner at his place.

I roll my eyes. "Laurie, that's just code for 'come over so we can fuck after you try to eat my awful excuse for a salad.' You know that, right?"

"You are mean." She chuckles. "At least I held him off last night. Tonight, maybe I don't care. Maybe I'm not going over there for the salad anyway."

I think of Brett, wondering if she'll regret what she's about to do, but it's not like I'm an expert. If I were, I wouldn't be here, my heart torn to pieces over Landon. "It depends on what you want. Just...don't get hurt."

She is silent. "I'm already hurt, Rach."

That makes me want to cry, for her, for myself. "I know," I reply.

"Oh well," she says with a long sigh. "How are you, really?"

"Not so good." Saying it out loud seems to remove the dam I've put on my feelings. "Laurie, it has to end. I can't do it anymore. It's just too hard. I don't trust him, I don't trust myself. I'm jealous, suspicious, insecure, and I hate myself for being so weak. I don't recognize myself anymore."

"Rach..." She sighs. "I don't know what to say."

"Yeah. I'm just..." I close my eyes. "I'm so unhappy."

There's a short pause. "So you want to leave him...again?"

I don't say anything.

"You can't keep running whenever you feel things aren't perfect, Rach."

"I'm not running. I'm going to tell him why we aren't working, and I'm going to make him understand that maybe it's best that we let each other go."

She snorts. "Will you tell him you're in love with him?"

I'm quiet, and I hear her sigh. "You've never faced up to admitting to him, or even to yourself, what you really want. What would make you less insecure, Rach? Him admitting to being in love with you too? Maybe he is. Maybe you both make it hard for yourselves. The truth is, relationships aren't always smooth sailing. Maybe the people around you have shielded you from their conflicts so much that you think love is always kisses and sunshine, but that's not the case. Sometimes you both have to work at it. It's when one or both partners are uninterested in doing the work that...you know, you call it quits." She sighs. "Tell him how you feel Rach. If you don't, he'll never know, and you'll always wonder what would have happened if you did. So, be honest. Find out for sure how he feels. Stop running. No matter what happens next, you can handle it."

After our conversation, I sit outside on the balcony, watching the sun set over the horizon. Could I really just tell him? I imagine the worst-case scenario—a rejection of my love—and it makes my body stiffen with dread and pain.

I can't bear that.

I imagine walking away again. I can do that, especially if he doesn't come after me to break down my weary walls with the promise of passion and pleasure.

But why would he, now that Ava is back in his life?

The sun turns a brilliant orange, burning up the clouds and sky in a final burst of vivid colors before it dies for the day. Inside the suite, the hotel phone starts to ring, and I leave the balcony to answer it. It's the people from the newly opened spa, asking if I'm ready for them. They arrive soon after, and I sit silently, my mind still in turmoil as my hair, nails, and makeup get the professional treatment.

Afterward, I go back to the bedroom to lay out my dress on the bed, then I put on my jewelry—a pair of deep sapphire drop earrings my parents gave me on my twenty-first birthday. The vibrant blue stones remind me of Landon's eyes, and there is another sharp pang of impending loss.

In the bathroom mirror, I stare at my reflection. My lips are a rich plum, my eyes rimmed with vibrant shadow and my lashes embellished with a mildly colored mascara. It's not a look I'm used to, but it's in line with the theme of the ball and with my dress. The hair stylist exclaimed with delight when she saw my hairpiece, and she styled my hair in an elaborate curl over one shoulder with the hairpiece glittering softly along the side of my head.

Making my way back to the bedroom, I'm surprised to find Landon in the dressing room, pulling on the jacket of his tuxedo. I watch him button it, not moving until he sees me in the full-length mirror in front of him. He turns around, his eyes taking me in, lingering on my face. He starts to come toward me, but then stops himself.

"You look incredible," he says.

"Thanks," I reply quietly. "I'll just put on my dress and I'll be ready."

He follows me to the bedroom, waiting as I lift the dress from the bed and slip it on, letting the folds slide over my body. I reach for the zipper, but Landon is already there. His hands flutter over my back as he zips me up. When he steps back and I turn to face him, I watch his chest swell.

"I..." He smiles tenderly. "I'm speechless."

The words are soft, almost like an entreaty. I blink rapidly, thinking how strange it is that suddenly everything makes me want to cry. I'm feeling raw with everything that seems so wrong with us, and yet, being here with him, it's the only thing I really want, the one thing I want more than anything else.

Even so, I'm not happy.

"Thank you." I smile up at him, blinking back tears. I watch uncomprehendingly as he drops to his knees, where my shoes are in a box on the floor. Slowly, with reverent care, he slips each one on my feet then rises.

"I'll be waiting outside," he says.

I watch him leave, admiring his beauty, desiring his love, and aching because I know that for my sanity, for any chance I can ever have at happiness, I'll have to let him go.

THERE IS A RED CARPET AND A BACKDROP AT THE entrance to the main lobby. I join Landon in smiling for the cameras and greeting guests, schooling my face into an expression of happiness that I don't feel.

The red carpet leads from the lobby to the ballroom, where the doors are thrown open to reveal the fantastical décor inside. Soft lights shimmer down from the ceiling, creating the effect of a moonlit night, flowers adorn the tables, and servers dressed as sprites and fairies drift around with trays. From somewhere, I hear the sound of running water blending seamlessly with the beautiful music coming from the orchestra.

"It's very beautiful," I whisper to Landon, awed beyond anything I expected to feel.

He squeezes my hand. "Thank you."

The guests are mostly distinguished people from all over the country. I recognize the famous faces, politicians, actors, musicians, tech billionaires, a posse of glamorous models...there are even a few people from Gilt. Everyone wants to talk to Landon, to congratulate him, and to ask questions. He keeps me by his side while he does what he does in public. He greets and engages his guests, his smile, voice, and mannerisms communicating his faultless manners, and also setting him apart from the people around him. It gives me a feeling like I'm the only one in the crowd who has access to the enigmatic man inside the suit.

"Took you long enough to get here." The words are warm and affectionate, a departure from the way he's been all night. I look in the direction he's facing and see Aidan grinning widely. His tuxedo looks almost as good on him as Landon's, and he wears it with an air of charming insouciance. He approaches us and pumps his brother's hand. "God! It is lovely," he exclaims, looking around. "You did it again. I'm sorry I'm late."

Landon is smiling. "I'm just glad you're here."

"Last minute issues with the play," Aidan replies before turning to me. "Didn't hurt that he had a plane waiting for me," he says, hugging me lightly and dropping a kiss on my cheek. "It's good to see you, Rachel."

"Same here," I reply, really happy to see him. "You look good."

"Ha!" He laughs. "Desperate damage control before leaving the plane. You should have seen me escaping New York and those horrible rehearsals. I looked like a fugitive."

We both laugh, and when I turn to Landon and my eyes meet his, he has a thoughtful expression on his face. I incline my head, curious, but just then, someone approaches him and he turns away to give them his attention.

Aidan continues to entertain me with anecdotes from the theater. When I ask him about Elizabeth McKay, the beautiful young star of his play, his face clouds and he changes the subject. Again, I start to wonder if there is more to his seeming dislike for that particular girl.

Another person approaches us just as the man conversing with Landon walks away. The new arrival is a woman, none other than Ava Sinclair. I spotted her earlier, across the room, standing out like a swan among the other socialites. She looks ravishing in a stunning black gown, her hair in an elaborate hairdo set with jeweled pins and her lips, a dark striking red.

She takes Landon's hand and smiles up at him before leaning forward to whisper something in his ear. There's a white flash as one of the press people takes advantage of the moment to take a picture. *Why wouldn't they?* I think unhappily. As a couple, they look incredible.

"Ava Sinclair." Aidan's voice is a mocking drawl, sounding more mature than his years. "I never thought I'd see this face again."

She looks at him, a hint of dislike in her eyes, then she smiles. "It's been ages, hasn't it?" She smiles at me and wiggles the fingers of one perfectly mani-cured hand. "How d'you do, Rachel?"

I smile back. "Wonderful, thank you." I pause, and then add politely, "You look great."

Her brows go up. "Well, so do you."

I smile inwardly. I have no intention of allowing her supercilious attitude to get to me. If there's really anything going on between her and Landon, then I won't stand in their way. I won't fight for something or someone I don't even know for sure belongs to me. "I was just thinking that it's such an enchanting event you all put together."

She smiles sweetly. "Were you? We did have a great time arranging it all." She gives Landon a sly smile before gliding off, her whole bearing elegant and almost regal. I stare after her, wondering how bad it would look if I abandoned my decision to ignore her cattiness and dumped my glass of champagne in her hair.

As if he can guess what I'm thinking, I feel Landon's fingers curve around my waist. "They should announce dinner any minute," he says.

Aidan nods. "And then after the boring speeches, some dancing." He looks at me. "I'm looking forward to seeing what you can do."

Pushing Landon and Ava out of my mind, I give Aidan a grin. "Game on."

They announce dinner soon after. We are all at the same table—Landon, me, Aidan, some members of the board of the Shelter Project and their partners and dates. Ava is with us also, but she's alone.

She's seated on Landon's other side, like a constant reminder that she is one of the big unanswered questions in our relationship. I try not to bristle as she engages his attention again and again. Instead, I concentrate on Aidan, listening to his jokes and joining him in conversation with some of the others at the table.

After dinner, Landon goes up to give a short speech about the Gold Dust, the history, the refurbishment, and his decision to work with the Shelter Project. He mentions some of their successes around the country and how he hopes the gala will raise enough to make a real difference. There will be an auction, he announces, naming some of the exclusive items he and other sponsors of the Shelter Project have donated. He is in turn serious, then smiling, his voice low, almost sensual, with an appealing cadence that makes it impossible not to listen to him.

I watch him with rapt attention, unable to look away. I want to tell myself that he's mine. I want to believe it. I want it to be true with every single fiber of my being.

"He's wonderful, isn't he?" Ava leans over

Landon's seat toward me, her voice a low murmur only I can hear.

I contemplate her face for a short moment. "You already know that," I reply.

She chuckles then looks over at Landon. "How do you women bear it? Holding on to him, even when you know that at best it's only for a little while, and soon you'll have to let him go."

I look her squarely in the eyes. "How did you bear it?"

Her smile widens. It's a self-satisfied, almost catlike smile. "Oh, it was never like that with us. He was so in love with me. I suspect he still is. No matter how many times I walked away from him, he always came for me. I believe I broke his heart when I eloped for my first marriage, but the reunion after my divorce..." She chuckles. "It was worth it. It's been worth it every time to come back to find him still waiting."

Still waiting. It makes sense. Maybe I was wrong to imagine that he didn't commit to the women before me because of some aversion to love, because of the scars from his childhood. Maybe he was simply waiting for the woman he really loves.

My eyes go to Landon on the stage. He's still talking, but his eyes are on me. My heart tightens, with desire, hopelessness, love... I swallow. "Good for you,"

I tell Ava, my voice slightly shaky. The room erupts into applause as Landon finishes his speech and hands the podium over to one of the board members of the charity.

There are more speeches, then the auction. A musician has donated a private concert, someone else a cask of rare wine. Landon's donation is a special edition chronograph, which goes for more than a million dollars.

When the auctions are over, the music kicks up a notch and Aidan takes my hand. "Still up for the challenge?" he asks.

"Of course." I follow him away from the tables. A pop singer is doing a rendition of one of her hits over the sound of the orchestra, and on the dance floor, guests are already moving to the music. I follow Aidan's lead, responding to his catchy exuberance and letting go of my inhibitions.

"Wow," he says after three songs. "You could dance circles around some professionals on Broadway."

"Oh, you flatter me sir," I reply theatrically. We both laugh. My laughter is cut short when I look back toward the tables and I see Landon and Ava, still seated. They're leaning toward each other, talking.

Aidan follows the direction of my gaze and snorts. "She's trying really hard."

I don't reply. To me, it looks as if she really isn't trying so hard. He's there with her, after all. I grab a flute of champagne from a passing server and down large gulp.

"Another dance?" I ask Aidan, my voice bright.

"Anything you want."

Landon cuts in a few minutes into our dance, just as the singer starts a slow, soulful rendition of one of her hits. Aidan hands me over to his brother with a cheerful nod and disappears into the party.

Landon's hands encircle my waist, and I place my hands on his shoulders, trying and failing to make myself immune to his raw sensuality. We're barely moving, just swaying gently to the mellow music.

"Are you enjoying yourself?" he asks.

I shrug. "Aidan has been excellent company."

It's a dig, and he recognizes it. His lips lift in a small smile. "I'm glad you two like each other."

"What's not to like? You know I think he's great."

He nods, and I look away from his face, ignoring the temptation to lean into him and place my head on his chest, to feel his warmth and the steady rhythm of his heart, to close my eyes and immerse myself in him alone.

I hear him breathe and feel his chest expand. "Rachel," he starts. "What happened earlier in the suite..."

I close my eyes, remembering our fight. The things he said, the things I said...and then I remember Ava, that maddening, confident smile. "Not now, Landon."

"No, I..." He stops. "I haven't stopped thinking about it. Your being here means a lot to me, Rachel. I hate the idea that I hurt you. I don't... I'm sorry for not trusting you about Jack."

"You already said that," I reply without looking at him.

He sighs, and his fingers move lightly on my waist. A small shudder rocks through me at the slight touch and I swallow. "I want us to work," he says gently. "I want—"

"Landon," I interrupt. His words are only breaking my heart because I've already decided what I'm going to do. I decided long before we came down for the party, and watching him with Ava only strengthened my resolve. "We don't work," I say gently. "We just don't work."

I feel his body freeze. "You're wrong."

"Am I?" My voice is soft. "I don't think so, Landon." *I can't bear the pain*, my heart screams silently. *I can't bear loving you like this*. When it comes to him, I'm always going to be insecure. I'm always going to be dreading the moment when he'll walk away from me.

"Don't do this again." There is a plea in his voice, a desperation in his touch. "For God's sake don't do this again."

"Why not? What does it even mean to you that I stay? It's just sex, Landon. Apart from that, we have nothing."

His jaw moves. "We talked about this, and you said you wouldn't walk away."

I close my eyes. Somewhere inside, I hoped he would tell me I was wrong, that what we have is more than sex, and that he feels something for me. Blinking back tears, I look up into his face. "I'm not walking away. I'm trying to make you see that we don't have a chance." *Not when I'm desperately in love with you and you don't feel the same.* I sigh. "You don't trust me. I don't trust you. We don't have anything to build a relationship on. Maybe it's best if we both walk away."

His eyes close. When he speaks again, his voice is bitter. "Tony will arrange for your transport. You can go any time you want.

My hands drop from his shoulders. "Landon—"

"No," he interrupts. His hands come up to cup my face. "Whatever it is you're looking for, Rachel, I hope you fucking find it."

He walks away, leaving me feeling as if my heart has been ripped out. I watch his retreating back, almost unable to breathe. I see someone approach him. I watch them start to talk. He laughs at something the person says, and that, to me, is like a blow. It's as if he has already relegated me to his past.

Someone approaches me with a smiling friendly face, wanting to dance, and I realize I'm still standing on the dance floor. I shake my head and walk woodenly to the edge of the room.

Aidan is dancing with a lovely girl in a pink dress. He sees me and waves. I wave back, feeling sick.

You can leave any time you want.

The clear dismissal replays in my mind. I watch Landon continue to navigate the room, watch him talking and laughing. I watch as Ava approaches him and they dance a slow dance. That's when I decide that I need to leave. I make my way to the doors, numb, moving past the few people already leaving. I make my way to the elevators, wishing as I leave the sounds of the party behind that it was somehow possible to shed all my feelings and memories as well.

CHAPTER 16

*Y*OU *can leave any time you want.*

The words follow me back to the suite, like an evil, taunting chorus in my head.

My hands are shaking as I undress. I toss the dress and accessories in my suitcase. I don't know what I'm going to do. I want to leave. I want to go somewhere far away, somewhere with no link at all to my life as it is now, where I would have the slightest chance of forgetting about Landon.

In the bathroom, I put on a robe and scrub the makeup off my face. My eyes stare back at me, wide and peaked, aching from the effort of trying not to cry.

We can't work. I always knew that. I knew it the

last time I walked away, but I was so weak, I let him draw me back into this...whatever it was we had. Now I'm going to go through the hurt of losing him again. What option do I have? I can't separate my emotions from the reality of our situation, just as he can't be the man I want him to be. I could never be sure he was all mine.

I return to the bedroom, but I stop at the door. Across the room, Landon is standing at the doorway from the hall, looking at my suitcase on the bed. He lifts his eyes to mine, and the pain there slices through my chest. "You're actually leaving," he states, as if he didn't quite believe it before.

I close my eyes. "Yes."

A few seconds of silence pass. I imagine the party downstairs, winding down without him. I wonder if he'll try to stop me, and if I'll have the strength to resist him.

"When do you want to go? Tonight?" His voice is suddenly dispassionate. "Have you called Tony?"

I shake my head.

"I'll let him know you want to leave. He'll have a plane waiting for you for whenever you're ready. His eyes go to my suitcase again. "Do you want me to leave?" he says. "I can arrange for another suite if you'd rather not have me around."

I shake my head, fighting an overwhelming urge to cry. "No...don't. You don't have to go."

He nods and walks away without another word, leaving me trembling. Will he leave now? Go back to join the party? Maybe end up somewhere with Ava...

I sit on the edge of the bed, my head in my hands. I'm so confused. On one hand, I know I'm doing the right thing, for myself, even for him.

But on the other hand...

Tears fill my eyes. My mind flashes with all the moments of tenderness from the past two weeks, every moment when he made me fall deeper and deeper in love with him.

Tell him how you feel.

My mind recoils from the idea. I hear Jack's voice in my head, the day I told him I loved him all those years ago, the brutal dismissal with which he rejected me.

I'd die if that happened with Landon. I just know that something inside me would wither and die.

If you don't tell him, he'll never know.

And I'll always wonder. I breathe. I need to be brave. If I tell him and he rejects me, then I won't be able to fool myself anymore. I'll have to move on because there'll be no other alternative.

Outside the bedroom, the hall is empty, and so is

the other smaller bedroom in the suite. The living room is also empty, dark and silent.

I start to panic, imagining him going to spend the night somewhere else, with someone else.

Then I notice the breeze and the curtains billowing from the open doorway to the balcony.

I approach uncertainly, suddenly not sure about what I want...what I have to say. Pushing the curtains aside, I step out into the cold night air. Landon is standing by the balustrade. He's no longer wearing his jacket, and his shoulders are broad but hunched in his white dress shirt. He has a drink in one hand, his face turned toward the many lights of the city.

As I watch, he raises the glass to his lips then places it carefully on top of the balustrade. He makes a sound like a sigh, and then straightens and runs a hand through his hair. He looks dejected, and so alone that it's heartbreaking to watch. I take a deep breath.

"Landon." My voice is so low, I'm surprised he hears it.

He turns so fast, his face coming alive with intense emotion that disappears in the space of a second. He turns back around without saying a word, and I watch as he picks up his glass again and takes a long drink.

I take a step forward, but his voice stops me.

"What do you want?" He sounds as cold as ice.

"I have..." I falter. "I wanted to talk."

His laugh is mocking and bitter. "You've already said it all. We don't work." He turns to face me again. "What else is there to say?"

"Landon..."

He shakes his head. "Stop, Rachel. Just stop it." His eyes hold mine, intense and burning. "I'm done," he says. "I'm sick of the mixed messages, the drama..." He laughs again. "You always have an excuse to walk away, no matter what I do. I get the message now. You've proven beyond any doubt that you're out of my reach." He sighs. "You really should leave," he says. "I intend to get well and truly drunk tonight."

He starts to turn away, his hand reaching for the glass again.

"I love you." The words burst out of my lips, soft enough that I can almost convince myself I didn't say them, but loud enough to make Landon stop in his tracks. He turns slowly, facing me with an uncomprehending frown. I close my eyes, and when I open them again, he's still looking at me. My heart is pounding, my chest heaving as I search his face for a reaction, waiting, hoping, praying I won't regret what I've just done.

"I love you," I repeat, slower this time. "I'm in love with you." I look away from the blaze in his eyes, my gaze falling to his chest. "I have since that week we spent together. I...I didn't want to fall in love with you, and I didn't plan to, and it has hurt..." My voice breaks, but I continue. "It has hurt every day, knowing you don't feel the same way." I meet his eyes again. He looks as if he doesn't understand what I'm saying. I swallow. "I just...I thought it would be easier if I let you go."

His brow is creased. I breathe, unnerved by his silence, by the lack of a reaction. "I didn't want something that at best was just a prolonged hookup, and now I don't want a relationship that has no chance of becoming something more, because I won't be able to bear it."

His eyes close, and my heart breaks as I feel the wave of regret emanating from him. This is where he'll tell me that he's sorry, that he doesn't feel the same. I clench my fingers; at least I've told him how I feel. Whatever happens from here on out, it's up to him.

"You don't have to say anything," I say softly, even though my heart feels shredded. I didn't expect him to tell me he felt the same way, but the reality hurts. It hurts so much.

But I've bared my heart to him, and the pretense is gone, along with the weight of having to live a lie every second I spend with him. I no longer have to pretend that what we have is enough. Even if I lose him now, I won't blame myself.

"I'm not asking anything from you," I continue. "I already know how you feel about commitment. I just wanted you to know the truth. I love you. That's the only reason why I ever walked away. I knew it was the only way I would have a chance to get over you. "

His eyes are still closed, and I wonder if he'll say anything. Maybe he won't. Maybe it would be easier for the both of us if I left now, instead of forcing him to acknowledge everything I've said. I start to turn back toward the door.

"Rachel..." I pause, surprised by the depth of emotion in his voice. His eyes are shiny as he takes a step toward me. "Don't go."

Don't go. I draw in a shaky breath. That's not what I want to hear, but it's something. My eyes fill. "Landon..."

"Don't go," he repeats. "Please."

I nod, then I take the few steps to where he's standing and wrap my arms around him. "I love you," I whisper again, strangely elated by saying the words out loud. "Nothing is ever going to change that."

I feel his chest expand, rising as he takes a deep breath. "You have no idea how afraid I am of hurting you."

I lift my face to his. I'm already hurting. I've been

hurting since the moment I realized I'd fallen in love with him. Could it ever hurt worse than it already has in the past, or worse than it does right now? I don't think so.

I place a soft kiss on his lips. "You won't," I whisper.

I feel him tremble. His hands come up to circle my arms, and they're shaking too. I pull back and smile sadly at him, memorizing all the lines of his face, every feature that I love.

"I love you," I whisper again, reaching up for another kiss. This time he kisses me back, his tongue stroking mine with a heat and urgency that makes me forget my pain. I run my fingers through the silky strands of his hair, filling my senses with his touch, giving in to my desire for him.

Landon releases my lips then holds me against his body for a long moment. I rest my head on his shoulder. *I'm glad*, I think fiercely. I'm happy and grateful for every single moment I've spent with him, and no matter what happens, I'll never regret it.

I raise my face to his. He still looks shaken, almost afraid, and in his eyes, I can see him struggling against whatever emotions are raging in his mind.

I stroke his hair. "Stop thinking," I urge gently.

He doesn't reply. I lift my lips and kiss him again. He sighs and raises his hand to my nape, kissing me back. I reach for the buttons of his shirt, undoing them so I can slide my hands over his chest.

"Rachel..."

I shake my head. I don't want him to hesitate. I want this. "Don't stop," I whisper.

He kisses me again, this time more deeply. I moan against his mouth as he undoes the tie of my robe, reaching inside it to stroke my heated skin. I shrug it off and press my body against his, not caring that we're out on the balcony. He's already hard against my belly and thigh. I grind against him and he groans, cupping my butt and lifting me off my feet.

I wrap my legs around his waist, letting him carry me inside, still kissing me. We make it to the living room before he lays me on the soft carpet, kneeling over me. He spreads my robe and leans down, drawing a nipple into his mouth and sucking deeply through the lace of my bra. My body arches in pleasure, lifting toward him. He slides one hand between my legs, palming me over my panties and rubbing me gently. My hips roll, my whole body clenching with the need for more.

I cry out when he moves his hand away, waiting breathlessly as he reaches behind me for the fastening of my bra and deftly removes the lacy undergarment. Then his hand slides back between my legs, inside my panties and between my folds, circling over my clit before sliding down to rim the entrance to my body.

The pleasure is intense. He lowers his head to my chest, licking the soft, sensitive skin of each breast before sucking on my nipples. I moan breathlessly, my skin misting with sweat as his touch drives me nearly insane.

Still touching me, he licks a path from my breast up to my ear. I feel his tongue on the underside of my earlobe, teasing and tasting. The pleasure brings tears to my eyes, and I reach for his face, pulling him close so I can suck on his lip. I thrust my tongue inside his mouth, trembling when he responds with a low groan.

He raises his head, and for a moment, he's just looking down at me. My eyes are unfocused with pleasure, especially when he chooses that moment to slide his fingers into my body, finding the most sensitive spot inside me and rubbing gently.

"What do you want me to do?" His voice is whisper soft. "What should I do?"

Through the fog of arousal in my brain, I know he's not asking about right now, but at this moment, all I want is to surrender myself to his touch.

"Don't stop touching me," I tell him.

His fingers plunge deeper inside me, spreading to stimulate my inner walls while his thumb circles my clit, massaging it until I can't take it anymore. His lips cover mine as I cry out, my body rippling with the pleasure of my orgasm.

Lost in my post-orgasmic haze, I don't remember much about being carried to the bedroom. I don't remember him undressing me or putting me under the covers, but I remember his voice in my ear as I fall asleep.

"Don't leave."

~

ANOTHER ONE OF LANDON'S NIGHTMARES WAKES me up. He's moaning, his hands digging into the pillow he's clutching tightly. The curtains are not fully drawn, and a little predawn light falls into the room from the soundproof windows, bathing his face with a muted light and showing me the tears glistening on his cheeks.

"Please," I hear him whisper. "Please."

I reach for him, gently stroking his hair. "Landon, wake up."

He reacts to my voice, a small frown appearing on his face. Slowly, his body relaxes and he opens his eyes. Intense relief washes over his features when he sees me.

"You're here," he breathes.

"I am," I say with a small smile.

He pulls me toward him, positioning me to lie on his chest, and then his arms come up around me. I relax into his warmth. "You were crying," I murmur. "Was it worse than usual?"

He is silent. I raise my head to look at him, waiting for an answer.

"It was you," he says quietly.

I frown. "I don't understand."

"It's always my mother," he says. "In the accident." He meets my eyes. "This time, it was you, and I couldn't save you."

I close my eyes. Of course he can't save me. His love could, but he can't give me that. "There's no accident." I sigh softly. "I'm fine. I don't need saving."

He looks as if he's about to argue. I shake my head and rise to my knees, placing one knee on either side of him. I take his face in my hands. "Stop torturing yourself," I tell him intently. "You're not going to hurt me. I'm going to be fine."

But am I? I push the doubts away as his hands close over mine, squeezing gently as he lifts them from his face. "I already have," he whispers.

I close my eyes. "Don't think about that."

He drops my hands and rears up so he's sitting on the bed. Then he pulls me down to sit on his lap, facing him. His hands trail down my arms while his eyes hold mine.

"Say it again," he says.

I know what he means. "I love you," I whisper.

His chest expands, and he buries his face in the space between my neck and my shoulder.

My arms go around his neck, and he starts to kiss me on my shoulder. I sigh and lean back, giving him the space he needs to lavish attention from my neck to my breasts.

I lower my head, nudging his face up so I can kiss him. His lips close over mine, kissing me deeply while my hands slide over his muscled arms and his firm back.

His hands grip my waist then slide up to cup my breasts, his thumbs working my nipples until I respond with a long moan. Then he starts to stroke my skin, from the sides of my breasts up to my shoulders and down my arms. He looks at me, and even in the darkness of the room, I can see his eyes, the conflict inside them. "I had no idea," he says.

"I know."

He kisses me again, and then with his hands on my back, he rolls over so I'm lying on the bed beneath him. Supporting himself on his elbows, he lavishes kisses on my face, my neck, and my breasts.

Pleasure shoots through me and I moan, heat

spreading between my legs. I thread my fingers in his hair, trailing one hand over his shoulder and back as he kisses his way over my stomach. His lips trail a hot path down to the center of my thighs then he nudges my legs farther apart. My whole body is pulsing with a wild burning desire, waiting for his touch, and when it comes, the pleasure is almost unbearable. He licks me, slowly, sensuously, his tongue moving across my folds, licking between them before moving up to circle sweetly around my clit.

My hips rock against his mouth, my hands gripping the sheet tightly. His tongue flicks around my clit, over and over, until I'm moaning uncontrollably. My body tenses, nearly over the edge, then his fingers are inside me, touching me with the expertise that knows exactly where to rub, where to stroke.

"Landon," I beg, not even sure what I want. "Oh God."

He continues, bringing me closer to climax. My body is writhing on the bed, possessed completely by the sensation of his tongue fluttering delicately on my clit. I can't think anymore as my brain shuts out everything but the intense pleasure. Heat spreads from my core, taking over my body. My hips start to buck and Landon grips my thighs, his tongue continuing the sweet torture as waves of pleasure wash over me.

I cry out his name breathlessly, begging him to stop, to continue—I don't really know. He releases my thighs and hovers over me, positioning himself and lifting my legs around his waist. Then he pulls me forward and pushes inside the sweet throbbing heat between my legs.

Helplessly aroused, I look up at him, luxuriating in the feeling of him inside me, in the fierce desire written across his features. His chest tightens, the muscles taut as he breathes deeply. Languidly, I reach up to run my fingers over the hard slabs of well-defined muscle, feeling them tense even further under my touch.

"You feel so good," he murmurs, his eyes closed. "So good." He slides deeper inside me then flexes his hips, pulling almost all the way out then pushing in again.

Gripping the tight muscles of his buttocks, I urge him deeper. He catches my hands at the wrists and leans forward to pin them on the bed. Bracing himself, he surges inside me again and I cry out, mindless with ecstasy. He picks up his pace, making love to me with an intensity that brings tears to my eyes while murmuring my name, over and over, like a fervent prayer in my ear.

Pleasure floods me again, leaving me moaning and straining beneath him. There's something so primal and unrestrained in the way he fucks me, like nothing else matters, and truly it doesn't. His hips rock as he thrusts inside me, deeper each time, the intense pleasure between my legs spreading over my core, my thighs, my belly...

I let out a helpless cry, my insides pulsing uncontrollably as my climax rocks me. Landon groans, his eyes locked on mine. He comes with a harsh unrestrained groan, thrusting all the way inside me as he spills himself hot and pulsing into me.

When he goes back to sleep, there are no more nightmares. I doze for a little while too, and when I get up, he's still asleep. I take a quick shower and dress silently, careful not to wake him. He looks relaxed and almost at peace, and it's excruciating to leave him lying there, but that's what I have to do.

It only takes a few moments to gather my things. I take one last look at him before I walk away. *I love you*, I whisper silently. If we're ever going to have a chance, then I have to let him find me. I have to let him decide if he can return my feelings.

If he can love me, he will find me.

I close my eyes and steel myself, and then I turn my back on him and walk away.

LOST IN YOU

For more information on LOST IN YOU, the next and final book in this series, go to www.serenagrey.com.

If you want to get an email when the next book comes out, subscribe to my mailing list at www.serenagrey.com/alerts.

I love reviews, so if you leave one on Goodreads and one of the book purchase sites, I'll be forever grateful.

Serena is obsessed with books. She reads everything—history, the classics, novels, poetry and comic books, and writes because the stories in her head won't leave her in peace otherwise. She loves all kinds of fiction, but has a soft spot for love, romance, and that flush of pleasure that can only be found at the end of a beautiful love story.

When she's not reading and writing, she enjoys cocktails, coffee, TV shows, and has never gotten over her crush on Leonardo DiCaprio. If she had to choose between a good book and ice cream, she'd take both and make a run for it.

∾

To be the first to find out about new releases from Serena,
sign up for her Mailing List at
www.serenagrey.com/alerts

CONNECT WITH SERENA

Facebook: www.facebook.com/authorserenagrey

Twitter: @s_greyauthor

Goodreads: www.goodreads.com/serenagrey

Website: www.serenagrey.com

BOOKS BY SERENA GREY

A DANGEROUS MAN SERIES

Awakening: A Dangerous Man #1

Rebellion: A Dangerous Man #2

Claim: A Dangerous Man #3

Surrender: A Dangerous Man #4

UNDENIABLE

SWANSON COURT SERIES

Drawn to You

The Hooker

Addicted to You

Lost in You

Find at www.serenagrey.com/books

Made in the USA
Columbia, SC
28 February 2019